DECK Z

❖ THE TITANIC ❖

DECK Z

⊱ THE TITANIC ⊰

Unsinkable. Undead.

CHRIS PAULS
MATT SOLOMON

CHRONICLE BOOKS
SAN FRANCISCO

Pauls, Chris.
  Deck Z : the Titanic / Chris Pauls and Matt Solomon. -- 1. ed.
    p. cm.
  ISBN 978-1-4521-0803-2
  1. Titanic (Steamship)--Fiction. 2. Zombies--Fiction. 3. Virus
diseases--Fiction. 4. Epidemics--Fiction. 5. Paranormal fiction. I.
Solomon, Matt. II. Title.

  PS3616.A47D43 2012
  813'.6--dc23

                              2012021823

Manufactured in the United States of America

Designed by **EMILY DUBIN**
Illustrations by **LYDIA ORTIZ**

10 9 8 7 6 5 4 3 2

Chronicle Books LLC
680 Second Street
San Francisco, California 94107

www.chroniclebooks.com

DEDICATION

To our wives Heather and Katy for encouraging us to go write. And to Sarah Malarkey for trusting us to do this.

ACKNOWLEDGMENTS

Collectively, Chris and Matt wish to thank Victoria Skurnick, Daniel Greenberg, and Lindsay Edgecombe at the Levine Greenberg Literary Agency, Chronicle Books, Jeff Campbell, Emily Dubin, the good folks at Encyclopedia Titanica, Drew Niles for handing us the vector, The Onion, Amanda Veith, John and Jimmy Roach, Joe Garden, Jeff Perry, John Urban, Ron Dentinger, and Barriques (Fitchburg and Middleton).

Chris would like to thank Heather Sabin, Dale, Susan, Todd, Heather, Carter, Jackson, Kenny & Dorothy Pauls, Camilla, Don, Dennis, Linda, Andy, Megan, Doug & Kathy Smith, Joe, Jan & Kira Sabin, Matt, Shandra, Ed & Diane Fink, Alex & Kyonghui Wilson, Jerard Adler, Blake Engeldorf, Tom & Meghan Hendricks, Chris & Kathy Briquelet, Ryan & Katy Pettersen, Mark & Keri Braithwaite, Rich & Keri Modjeski, Dan & Amy Turner, Marc Schwarting, Rob & Max Wheat, Angela Keelan Martinez & Jesus, Jon McCorkle, Brooke Dobbs, Adam Goodberg, Chris & Becky Henkel, Debra Spector, Mark Murray, Mark and Karen Kampa, Shawn Quinn, John Hageman, Scott Sherman, Janet Ginsburg, Anita Serwacki, Dan Guterman, Joe Nosek, Doug Moe, Jim Johnson, Neil Spath, Scott Neu, Tom Oberwetter, Rich Hamby, Kirk Bosben, Bill Jackson, The Three Kings, The Cash Box Kings, Knuckeldrager, Karma to Burn for "Twenty," and as always, everybody at The Village Bar.

Matt wishes to thank Jake, Ben, and Sammi for giving me a reason to get up in the morning, Jerry and Connie for teaching me to work hard and love books, and Joe and Greeg for staying out of my room. Extra-monster thanks to those of you who pushed me forward: Judy Santacaterina and Matt Swan, the Prom Committee and Madison CSz, Jay, Yi and Tha, Ken and Jill, Julie, Ted, and Jack, Colleen, Maddie, and Emma, Michele Laux, the Nygores, the Kollmans, Patricia Ohanian Lundstrom, Halsted Mencotti Bernard, the freaks in San Diego, and the Mothership Connection.

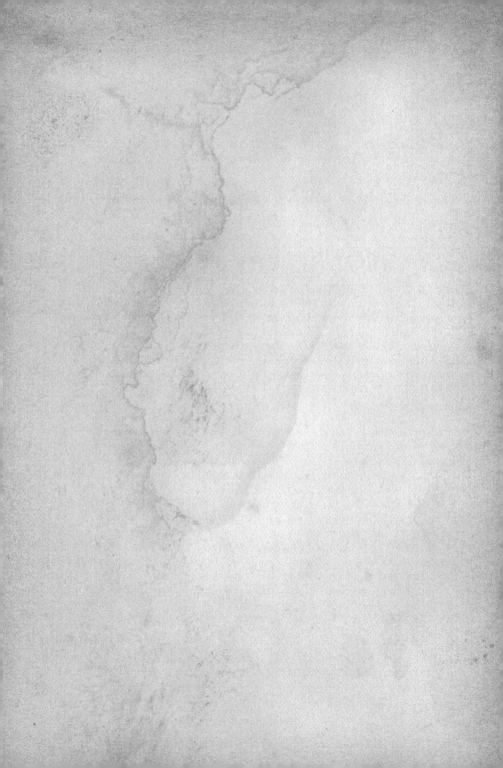

"Where men are the most sure and arrogant, they are commonly the most mistaken, and have there given reins to passion, without that proper deliberation and suspense, which can alone secure them from the grossest absurdities."

DAVID HUME,
AN ENQUIRY CONCERNING THE PRINCIPLES OF MORALS

PROLOGUE

"Over there."

A man in a stylish red jacket pointed to the right side of the convex window in the MIR deep-sea submersible as it hovered over the ocean floor, two and a half miles below the surface.

"Those boots," the Man in Red said, pointing to a half-buried pair at the edge of the sub's halogen lights. "Right there. I need those. Grab them for me."

"We need to be on our way," said the sub pilot. "My next group is waiting topside."

For two hours and twelve minutes, the submersible had passed alongside the forlorn, broken corpse of the *Titanic* and over its massive debris field, and that was exactly twelve minutes longer than had been paid for.

"This will be the last thing. Besides," the Man in Red protested, "this is important historical work."

A third man wearing a blue fleece shifted uncomfortably, coughed, and addressed the Man in Red. "I'll say it again: when I agreed to share this sub with you, I didn't expect to join a salvage mission. There's no scientific value in plundering *Titanic* for china and old bottles of champagne. This is show business, what you're doing."

"Just the boots, please," insisted the Man in Red to the sub pilot.

The pilot sighed and guided the sub to the right, extending the submersible's arm as he went.

"*Titanic* should be studied, not disturbed," grumbled the Man in Blue.

"No," the Man in Red argued. "History should be shared with the living."

The sub glided to a halt in front of the boots, and the pilot manipulated the crane arm. The deft metal fingers closed on a heel and pulled it from the silt: it was a woman's boot, tall, made to lace up over the calf, though the laces were long gone.

The Man in Blue felt his stomach turn. Even though he knew better, he half-expected to see the remains of a leg inside. But as the shoe was raised, only sand emptied out in a billowing cloud. "Those boots you're taking," the Man in Blue said. "They belonged to a real woman, you know. A real flesh-and-blood human being who died tragically. How is this any different than digging up a grave?"

"Whoever died in those boots is long gone." The Man in Red's voice was even, indifferent. "The boots are artifacts now. People can learn from them."

"Couldn't you photograph or videotape these *artifacts* in their natural environment?"

"I could, but what's more powerful than holding the past in your hand?" The Man in Red smirked: in fact, the boots were worth their weight in gold, perhaps more than all the cutlery and dinnerware he'd gathered so far. The boots conjured the lady who once wore them, and that's what drew exhibit audiences.

"This is stealing, plain and simple. You're a profiteer. You and your whole traveling road show. I'm here to expand scientific knowledge by studying new forms of life."

"You mean those rusticles, or whatever you call them? That's life, I suppose." The Man in Red waved his hand. "And you'll no doubt profit from your discoveries, too, as much as you can. But is there nothing to learn from history? This recovery of artifacts is called 'historical preservation.' The federal courts agree, in case you'd care to take it up with them."

For the second time, the crane arm disappeared from sight beneath the window, inserting the mate of the first boot into a holding compartment in the belly of the submersible.

"Done," the sub pilot grunted. "Now we surface."

"Wait!" exclaimed the Man in Red.

"We're finished!" the sub pilot growled back. "You've got your boots."

"No," the Man in Red commanded. He pointed to a metallic tube just beyond where the boots had lain. The cylinder, half-buried and sticking up at an angle, glinted in the halogen lamp's bright light. It was odd, unusual; to his practiced eyes, the Man in Red could tell this wasn't some casual everyday item. The tube held, or once held, something important—and good mysteries sold even more tickets. "We're not leaving without that. I'll pay another ten thousand."

The pilot hesitated. His daughter, a senior in high school, was starting college that fall. "Fifteen."

"Done. I'll wire the money after we surface."

"This is wrong!" exclaimed the Man in Blue, as the brooding presence of the ghostly ship loomed. "You don't even know what that is!"

Neither the sub pilot nor the Man in Red responded. The crane arm extended and pinched the tube successfully between its stiff, gray fingers, then retracted slowly, drawing the tube from its century-old resting place. Only once his prize was aboard did the Man in Red turn to speak.

"Solving mysteries like this tube is how we learn from the past. It could be anything. The deed to an old English estate. A treasure map. Perhaps only a giant cigar. It doesn't really matter. Each item is a window into another time. It's how we keep the dead alive."

STAGE ONE

1

Theodor Weiss rose from a finely crafted oak rocking chair to retrieve
the remaining hunk of spruce from the room's wood box and place it
in the cast-iron Franklin heating stove. Shafts of light from the setting
sun beamed through the chalet's window as particles of dust swirled
through the golden air in his wake. A fresh supply of logs was stacked
outside, but he wouldn't need them. He opened the stove door. A
comforting wave of heat blew forth. After the events of the past year,
he would always be grateful for warmth.

During the previous winter of 1910–11, a plague epidemic in Manchuria had overwhelmed Chinese authorities, forcing them to send out
a worldwide plea for help. Eleven nations dispatched their top bacte-
riologists; Germany had sent Weiss. Upon arrival in Mukden, a city
devastated by the epidemic, he suffered the bitter, minus-thirty-degree-
Fahrenheit cold, and he witnessed the death. Both were inescapable.

Weiss and the other international experts did what they could for
the sick, but none of the infected survived. Efforts turned to understanding the plague's nature, and Weiss was hailed by the Chinese
government for determining the plague to be pneumonic, rather than
the typical bubonic variety that was spread by rat fleas. It was a form
of pestilence not seen since antiquity.

The epidemic was largely over by spring thanks to strict quarantine measures, but the outbreak had killed nearly fifty thousand people. Afterward, Weiss remained in Manchuria to research the plague's origin, and in late January of 1912, he received a cable from Kaiser Wilhelm II himself:

Chinese government has requested your assistance investigating potential outbreak of new plague. I have agreed. Two officials from our Interior Department already in Manchuria to study anti-plague measures. They will join you.

The Chinese were very concerned about a report from a fur trader in Manzhouli, who had encountered a primitive tribe of reindeer herders called the Evenki. Until then they had only been known to be peaceful. Two of the nomads had attacked the trader, or so he claimed, and tried to tear into his flesh with their teeth. As far-fetched as it sounded, he said only the tough hide of his jacket and a fast horse saved him. The herders appeared very ill, with darkened blood running from their mouths, noses, and most disturbing of all, eyes. The fur trader felt lucky to escape with his life.

Having seen firsthand what Manchuria endured only months earlier, Theodor Weiss would have felt obligated to do what he could even without an order from the Kaiser.

Six men set out into the western Manchurian wilderness in search of the Evenki. Weiss, two Chinese medical officials, and a guide sat substantially lower in their saddles than the strapping Germans from the Interior Department. The junior and senior German officials, both straight-backed, no-nonsense types, took turns riding ahead of the pack with the guide.

Eventually, they found a small Evenki encampment with only a dozen dwellings circled in a forest clearing. A herd of reindeer paced nervously in a makeshift pen. A village elder appeared and warned them away. Speaking with the elder in his native tongue, the guide explained that the strangers were there to help. He indicated that Weiss was a powerful healer. The weathered elder consented and led the party into the village.

One hut stuck out among the others, surrounded by tall pikes adorned with carvings of birds. Muted drumming wafted with smoke from the hut's conical top. The guide said the hut was home to the tribe's female shaman.

As in Mukden, Weiss changed into a one-piece gown, with goggles, gloves, and a special mask that allowed him to safely examine plague victims. It was his own design. The elder held back the hut's tanned flap for Weiss to enter. The others waited outside.

Inside the hut's dim firelight, the shaman huddled on the ground over a drum, pounding a hypnotic rhythm. A central fire crackled with iridescent colors and filled the air with aromatic smoke. The shaman stopped playing and rose. She was dressed in a fur cloak, a menacing white mask, and gloves. The mask's dark, recessed eyes hovered above a gaping red mouth, and lengthy feathers stuck out from the top. The shaman gestured Weiss closer. The impossibly long fingers of her white gloves seemed to grow like talons in the flicker of the fire.

Stepping aside, she revealed two men kneeling with their arms and ankles bound. They appeared young, in their early twenties, perhaps brothers, with strong bodies forged from their hard lives in the frigid wilderness. It was their faces that made Weiss's breathing apparatus pulse faster. A reddish, bleak fluid streamed from their mouths, noses, and eyes, just as the fur trader described. The men moaned continually, eyes focused in a catatonic state on the snapping fire.

Weiss recognized the dark sores and flushed skin he'd witnessed in Mukden, but this appeared to be a variation of the pneumonic and bubonic plagues. The men had progressed to such an extreme state it was a wonder they were still alive. From a pocket, Weiss removed a glass tube containing a sterile swab and uncorked it. He needed to collect a sample of that discharge.

Cautiously, Weiss edged closer, extending the swab. It broke the first man's focus. His eyes locked on Weiss, and the infected man lunged. His mouth opened wider than should have been possible, and he bit down on Weiss's shoulder before the German could react. Thankfully, the suit's tough material prevented the bite from breaking through.

Weiss desperately tried to push off the crazed villager, but his two front teeth were hooked over the top of Weiss's collarbone. The shaman jumped up to help Weiss and pulled him free with surprising strength. As she did, the second infected villager dove and sank his teeth into the base of her neck. It was the only exposed spot on the shaman's body, where her cloak ended and her mask began. Weiss kicked the attacker hard in the head, breaking his grip on the shaman. The two infected men writhed on their bellies, unable to rise because of the bindings, moaning and snapping wildly at the air.

The shaman slumped over. Her cloak hung to the side; a ragged wound marked her mauled neck. Weiss approached to inspect the injury, but the shaman waved him off. She reached for a leather pouch and pointed for Weiss to leave. As he crawled through the hut's opening, he watched her apply a thick salve to the wound.

Through the guide, Weiss explained to the Chinese authorities what had just happened: The two men inside the hut appeared to be infected with some variation of the plague, a strain completely unfamiliar to him. The sickness made them violent. Certainly, the fur trader's tale was confirmed. Weiss asked the village elder if he knew of any other Evenki so diseased. He said no.

The elder German official nodded thoughtfully. "Perhaps we have contained this disease just in time. Still, if it ever reached a populated area there would be mass chaos and destruction. We should study the infection, to learn everything possible in case of another outbreak."

"That would be too dangerous. We cannot allow such a thing," the Chinese official responded.

Weiss added, "I agree. And frankly, Manchuria's facilities aren't up to the task."

"We will protect the Fatherland and the world from this plague," said the German official. "We cannot walk away. I have the authority to commit German resources for such study. I will arrange transportation by rail so Professor Weiss can safely examine a subject in Germany's best laboratories."

Weiss considered the situation. The two men were beyond saving, but perhaps not the shaman if they could act quickly enough. The infected man's black mucus had stained her wound, and she would soon fall ill. However, the shaman was now the ideal test subject to study the course of this plague, even if she didn't live. What sort of mutation was this, and why had the men survived past the point when all other Manchurian plague victims were killed? Studying its effects in a living person could be the key to an effective treatment, if not a cure, perhaps one that could work for all strains.

The shaman emerged from the hut. Weiss addressed the guide: "Please tell her the bite may make her sick soon. If she comes with us, I can try to help her."

She nodded as the German's plan was conferred, then turned toward the group.

"She sees you as a powerful shaman," the guide said to Weiss. "The evil spirits were powerless against your costume. She will do as you say."

Weiss admired the shaman's bravery, though he wasn't certain she understood the gravity of her situation. He addressed the Chinese officials. "The men inside are beyond help. I recommend the two victims be dispatched. Burn their bodies, this tent, and everything in it. When that is done, the Evenki must move their camp. That should take care of the immediate threat here. The shaman will come with us by rail to Germany. I'll do all I can to help her."

The Chinese officials huddled, then gravely nodded their acceptance.

A plume of coniferous smoke escaped from the briefly open stove door and mingled with the aroma of coffee percolating on the stovetop. Anticipating a long night, Weiss poured himself another cup from the pot. His hands were perfectly steady, as they always were, no matter how much coffee he drank. Then he headed out the door into the cabin's one and only other room.

The long, narrow space was dark, and he quickly shut the door to keep it that way. A small amount of light snuck beneath the room's thick curtains, but until his eyes adjusted, the room seemed pitch black. He paused and blew across his coffee, standing next to a steel desk covered with papers. Past that were several laboratory-grade stainless-steel tables covered with beakers, test tubes, and burners, which stood next to three large gas tanks. A stench of rot and form-aldehyde stung the inside of his nostrils. Like the wood box near the stove, the formaldehyde tanks were nearly empty and would not need replenishing. He took a cautious sip of hot coffee, then set the cup down gingerly on the ghostly outline of the desk and walked deeper into the room.

Weiss didn't need light to find his way. He'd long ago counted the steps: twenty-three past his equipment, turn right for two steps, left for five steps, and then stop in front of the custom-made, six-foot-tall, thick-walled glass enclosure that anchored the end of the room. As he walked, he reached into his pocket and fingered his lighter, flicking open the top so it would be ready to go.

He walked slowly and silently; it was not yet time for haste. When he arrived in front of the glass cage, he paused to listen. No sound but the ticking of gauges. *Good.* With his left hand, he brought forth his lighter, and with his right hand, he lifted his sweater as if to guard the flame from a breeze. With calm deliberation, his thumb spun the abraded wheel across the flint and a single spark leapt onto the carefully trimmed wick. A thin, blue flame jumped forth.

He quickly began his work. On top of the enclosure, a galaxy of tubing emanated and flowed down the outside, its meandering course ending in a single 16mm by 150mm vial. A drop of jet-black fluid fell into the tube. It was nearly full, but he was determined to get every drop possible. The sound of movement from inside the glass, like cloth on cement, caused Weiss to smother the flame by snapping shut the lighter top with a practiced flip of his thumb. He thought he saw the figure inside turn toward him, but it made no more sound.

As Weiss silently retraced his steps, gathering his coffee and returning to his living room and the warmth of the stove, he thought: *The vial is ready. Now I wait only for darkness. It's time.*

2

The most prominent feature of Army Chief of Staff Helmuth von Moltke's wood-paneled study was an enormous map of Europe that hung on the wall. Arrows showed the potential paths of various armies and where they might meet if the German Empire found itself fighting a two-front war against both France and Russia. Indeed, Germany had long considered initiating just such a conflict. The map's battle plan was the brainchild of Moltke's predecessor, Alfred von Schlieffen, and it bore his name.

The Schlieffen Plan first circulated among German General Staff members in 1905, when the high command felt a war in Europe was inevitable. The strategy called for an initial strike and quick defeat of France in the west before radically turning east and shifting decisive force against Russia, which was historically slow to mobilize. For seven years Moltke had studied the Schlieffen Plan, and for seven years he had felt uneasy.

In his estimation, the gambit's success was predicated on the precarious notion that the "Russian Steamroller" would be unable to gain momentum fast enough. If any part of the initial campaign in France slowed the German Army, it could prove disastrous when the time came to engage Russia. Germany needed absolute assurance that the

Czar would not be able to marshal his forces in time, but the necessary strategy or ingredient had proved elusive.

Until now.

Moltke strode to a sideboard and lifted a decanter of brandy, pouring a celebratory draught of Weinbrand into a snifter. Suddenly, a figure emerged from behind him, and the decanter nearly slipped from his grasp. Moltke flinched, and then relaxed, trying to cover his shock with nonchalance.

"I should have known. How did you get in?"

The young man helped himself to the brandy snifter. He stood about six feet tall, with dark hair and plain features. His expression was inscrutable, and his civilian clothes were impeccable, dark, and neutral. He appeared both threatening and unassuming at the same time. With a lone gulp, he finished the brandy and set down the glass.

"I let myself in," he replied.

You've been trained well, Moltke thought. He refilled the glass and poured himself a second snifter, which he raised aloft. "To a new map," he said and drank. The man joined him in the toast.

"The time has come sooner than expected," Moltke said. "It's why I asked you here. We believe Weiss has finished with his work and is now only delaying. Tomorrow we will take what we need from him. You will leave this week with the vial."

The young man eyed Moltke curiously. "It's time for more details, Herr Moltke, about your weapon and of what it is you would have me do. What sickness would cause the Russians to mobilize en masse against it?"

Moltke regarded the young man in turn. "I suspect even you will quail at the sight of the horror it brings. And the Russians will respond just as I say—they'll exhaust their resources to end the threat." Moltke put a pen to the map and circled a city in Russia.

"Once we have the Toxic, you will take and release it here, in Perm. A week later, when Perm is in chaos, we will begin our attack of France, per the brilliant strategy of Herr Schlieffen."

For the first time, the younger man showed a flash of emotion. "*Perm* is the target? That's not what we agreed."

"Of course," Moltke replied, "Germany's strategic needs come before personal vendettas. By striking Perm, we eliminate a major munitions center and pin the Russian Army up against the Ural Mountains."

"And what happens to Kishinev?" The man pointed to a spot east of the Urals near the Baltic Sea. "How do I know the city will be destroyed if the plague is to be unleashed so far west?"

Moltke replied heavily, "I'll hear no such talk. *You* came to us. You're a member of the Imperial German Army now, and you'll take orders as such."

The young man tensed, his eyes never leaving Moltke's as he slowly placed his half-empty glass on the sideboard.

The Army Chief of Staff suppressed his anger at his subordinate's arrogant indifference to the chain of command. Moltke knew the man was the perfect agent for this important mission, a former Russian who could move undetected in Perm while infecting the city. Germany needed him.

Moltke's lower lip jutted out. "Consider Kishinev a secondary target. Continue there after assuring the infection is raging in Perm."

The pair eyed each other warily. A wild look inflamed the young man's face. "Kishinev must truly suffer for its sins."

Moltke smiled. "A few drops and Russia will burn Kishinev and everyone in it to the ground."

The Agent retrieved his glass and held it aloft. "Then let's drink to wiping Kishinev off the map."

3

Weiss fed the notes detailing his return trip from Manchuria into the heating stove, careful to destroy each page. Not one shred of his work could survive. Flames devoured a black-and-white photo of the shaman, still in tribal costume and bound to a cot inside a railway car.

The shaman's condition had deteriorated dramatically by the time they'd reached the Manzhouli railway. Despite her binds, the woman Weiss now referred to as "the Subject" was insatiably hostile. Weiss kept her shaman mask on, as protection against her aggression and to avoid becoming emotionally attached to the woman underneath.

The days went by with few words; the Interior Department officials had little to say to Weiss. The older one carried a deck of cards in his jacket and spent most of the journey taking money from his junior partner.

Traveling in a confined space with her agonized moaning was unbearable. It made a full night's sleep impossible. Near the end of the two-week trip, the younger Interior Department man, desperate for rest, tried to muffle her with a gag. If Weiss had been awake, he would have stopped him. The official pulled back her mask, and she viciously latched onto a chunk of his palm. His compatriot intervened, wrenching him free but not before the Subject also managed to bite the older man on the forearm. Her shrieks and the men's screams woke Weiss, but too late. The damage was done.

Weiss donned gloves, cleaned the Germans' wounds, and informed them that, most unfortunately, restraints would be necessary for the rest of their journey. The men protested, but Weiss appealed to their sense of German pride and duty. They witnessed what the Subject had become. Weiss promised that if, by some miracle, they weren't showing signs of disease within twenty-four hours, he would release them. The men relented and allowed themselves to be bound. Then Weiss did the only thing he could: closely observe their condition. His notes chronicled the men's descent through what seemed to be three fairly distinct stages. One page summarized his findings:

STAGE ONE: *Flu-like symptoms, headache, chills, intermittent nausea. Appears like early symptoms of the plague. The men describe a constant uncomfortable ache, and exhibit conscious self-awareness.* **Duration:** *approximately eight hours.*

STAGE TWO: *Murky, intermittent discharge begins to emanate from mouth, nose, and ears. Black, pox-type sores appear on skin. Headaches more severe. Periodic grabbing of the ears. Mental agitation increases. The men still speak, but not always intelligibly. Both pleaded with me to kill them.* **Duration:** *approximately three hours.*

STAGE THREE: *Discharge now flowing freely from eyes. Total loss of higher functions. Ability to communicate is gone. Vocalizations consist entirely of moaning. Demonstrate unbridled aggression toward sound or any human movement. They are no longer men.* **Duration:** *Unknown. None of the subjects have yet to die of the disease.*

When the train finally reached Berlin, Weiss was met by Helmuth von Moltke and a contingent of the German Imperial Army. With great regret, Weiss informed them of the tragedy that had occurred en route.

"Transport to a laboratory awaits you and your Subject," said Moltke. "We will take custody of the men and see they are put out of their misery."

Weiss was shocked that Moltke wanted him to continue in light of what had happened but agreed to keep the original Subject for study. Hopefully, a treatment or cure could be developed. Weiss insisted, however, that he needed to work in total isolation to avoid further tragedies. Moltke consented, in exchange for appraisal on all progress.

With meticulous care, a special glass enclosure was built to house and restrain the Subject in a two-room cabin on Brocken Mountain, the highest peak in the Harz range. From the top of the enclosure, Weiss could safely access the Subject, who seemed to need nothing to survive. Every three days, as had been arranged, Weiss hiked down to Schierke for supplies and to update Moltke on all progress and developments by post. Yet when Weiss returned to his cabin laboratory, he sometimes had a nagging feeling that someone had visited in his absence. On a hunch, he sent a note to a trusted contact in the Interior Department, inquiring about the infected men who had been taken off the train and destroyed.

As the weeks went by, Weiss struggled without success to find a bacterium similar to that which caused the bubonic and pneumonic plagues. He knew one had to be present and suspected that by the time the pathogen was transmitted, it was hiding within other cells.

One thing seemed clear: instead of proceeding to the lymph nodes or lungs, this particular plague form made its way to the brain. There, it nibbled away, causing the kind of violent madness Weiss had seen firsthand.

That theory gained credence when X-ray analysis revealed a dark, fluid-filled sac directly in the middle of the Subject's skull. Protected by the sac's defensive membrane, this was where the bacterium likely multiplied before sneaking into the blood that flowed out the nose, mouth, ears, or eyes. Weiss needed the pure strain of bacteria within the sac, and he designed an apparatus to drain the mysterious fluid he named "the Toxic."

Fitting the apparatus was the tricky part. He'd had to do it with all light extinguished to remove stimuli and calm the Subject. Even then, he'd nearly been bitten. In the dark, he removed her mask from above, then waited for the inevitable thrashing to subside. When it did, he affixed the umbilical halo of the drilling apparatus to her skull. Then, safely removed on the other side of the glass, he sparked his lighter and looked on her unmasked face for the first time. Even accounting for the awful ravages of the disease, she must have been old when she was infected, with lined skin and silver hair. Now the flesh on her face was so rotted that her cheekbones lay exposed. Her ragged, purple lips moved only because of her furiously masticating jaw. Despite age and advanced decay, the Subject remained frighteningly strong. Weiss wasn't a religious man, but he asked for forgiveness just the same. Then he pulled a lever to initiate the procedure.

His specially-designed probe descended from the halo, drilling straight down into the Subject's skull. She seemed to not feel a thing. Upon arrival at the sac, a titanium needle extended from the instrument and cleanly pierced the soft pouch. Drawing out the Toxic then commenced, very slowly, at the rate of a 1ml per day, so as to prevent collapse of the sac and possible leakage. He estimated it would take a month to get it all.

Lab work with early samples of the Toxic proved exciting beyond words. Within days, he'd had some limited success interrupting the pathogen's ability to create enzymes that protected it from antibodies.

Not a cure yet, but surely once he'd found the key, a treatment for other forms of the plague would follow in short order. It would be the culmination of a life's work.

Shortly after this breakthrough, Weiss finally received a return post from his Interior Department contact. The men who had joined Weiss in Manchuria hadn't been department officials after all. Following cremation, they had been given Imperial German Army military funerals.

After reading the letter, Weiss returned from Schierke to his cabin, only to find carefully concealed footprints in the snow outside. His suspicions seemed to be confirmed: the German Army was watching and manipulating him, as it had from the beginning. But why?

Only one reason seemed possible: They wanted his research and especially the Toxic, not for a cure, but to use as a weapon. When Weiss had told Moltke of the distillation being extracted, his return communiqué asked for a firm completion date, and now that appeared to reveal his true motivation. Weiss then wondered, *How long before he tries to seize my work?*

––––•––––

As the last page from the file ignited, Weiss shut the door to the stove. He picked up one of five gasoline containers and a lantern, then walked into the dark laboratory for the last time.

Arriving at the containment chamber, he set the gas down, lit the lantern, and braced himself for the Subject's reaction. All stayed still. He placed the lantern on the floor and removed the nearly full vial. After sealing the Toxic securely, he placed the vial in a larger, airtight metal cylinder with a padded interior. He stowed the tube, 250mm in length, in an unassuming, black leather valise and drew out an imposter vial filled with India ink. Weiss carefully inserted it in the Toxic's place. Then he thoroughly doused the apparatus in gasoline. The creature instantly raged.

Pausing for a moment in front of the chamber, Weiss's angular face reflected in the glass, reminding him of his twin sister, Sabine, her features faintly superimposed over his own.

With sudden ferocity, the Subject's exposed cheekbones and decayed nose slammed headlong into the glass barrier, driving Sabine's image back into Weiss's heart.

The Subject's savageness startled him, as it always did, and he nearly dropped his valise. She pounded her head wildly against the chamber, as if relentlessly beating on the gates of Hell. Weiss returned with two additional cans of gas and emptied them throughout the lab. When finished, he stood next to the chamber and put a hand against the glass.

Weiss felt a terrible pang of grief. The Subject had once been human, a shaman, dedicated to healing others just as he was. Even when doomed to die, she'd sacrificed herself to become part of his work. He pushed aside sentimentality. He could not save the dead, but with the Toxic, there remained hope for the living.

"Thank you," he said.

Smoke from Weiss's cigarette wound into the gathering fog surrounding the top of snowy Brocken Mountain, eventually becoming part of its shrouding mist. Valise in hand, he leaned on a walking stick twenty yards from the chalet, which would soon be completely engulfed in flames.

He knew he should hurry, but he wanted to ensure that the entire structure, and everything in it, burned. How long did he have before the German Imperial Army personnel undoubtedly below in Schierke were alerted to the blaze raging just within the Brocken's tree line? He hoped the early hour would buy him extra time.

His actions made him a marked man. If he were captured, the best he could hope for was life imprisonment. More likely, it would mean a firing squad. He checked the safety on his pistol and returned it to the vest pocket of his jacket.

Smoke poured and billowed from every crack and seam in the cabin. A window shattered, and flames leaped out, taking great gulps of air and greedily licking the eaves before spreading to the roof. Weiss took one last drag from his cigarette and was suddenly knocked to the ground as the building exploded.

He sat up, disoriented, brushing snow and embers from his overcoat. His ears were ringing. *There was more formaldehyde left in those tanks than I thought*, he cursed to himself, slipping as he scrambled to his feet. The valise had flown from his hand and lay a few yards away. He rushed to it and pulled out the cylinder. A close inspection of the vial inside revealed no damage.

Now Weiss moved with urgent purpose. He faced a nearly two-hour hike down the dark mountain. He'd only descended a hundred feet when the German skidded to a stop. Ahead in the mist, an impossibly tall, black, ghostlike figure stood at the forest's edge, crowned by a glowing halo. To steady himself, Weiss dug his walking stick deep into the snow. The menace matched his movement, and as it did, Weiss recognized the vision for what it was.

The blaze raging behind him and the surrounding fog were conducive to producing a *Brockengespenst*. The specter ahead was actually his shadow landing on billowy air moisture, an optical illusion seen throughout the ages by climbers on the Brocken. He waved a hand and the *Brockengespenst* waved back. Weiss grinned momentarily, let out a deep breath, and resumed his descent.

The sound of a low moan compelled him to stop once more.

Weiss wheeled around. A flaming body lumbered erratically just up the incline. Released by the explosion, the Subject was now a blazing abomination. The smell of burning human hair and reindeer hide—the shaman's cloak—filled the air.

He stabbed his walking stick into the snow and pulled the gun from his vest. Sighting carefully, he fired at the Subject's chest.

Flames burst in all directions as the bullet plowed into the Subject's body and escaped through the other side. The Subject seemed unfazed, except that now it spied Weiss and emitted a rising moan as it staggered toward him. Weiss fired recklessly at the advancing creature. Again and again bullets struck the body until the hammer found no more cartridges, clicking uselessly. Weiss tossed the gun aside and grabbed the only other weapon available: his walking stick. He could probably outrun the damaged wreck of a being, but it could not be left alive—if such a thing could be called living. Somehow, it had to be destroyed.

Weiss waited for the Subject to advance closer. He could feel the heat from its still-burning flesh as he leveled the stick and rammed it hard into the midsection. The Subject stumbled, then lost its balance and careened awkwardly down the mountain, bouncing off trees along the way until landing with a muffled thud just out of Weiss's sight.

No sound filled the night save the crackle of the burning cabin. Weiss crept down the mountain, finding the Subject's body at the foot of a snowy outcropping. He relaxed. The Subject had spun headfirst into a jagged granite boulder and cracked its skull in half.

The body still burned, but Weiss took no chances. He pawed the forest floor for dry pine boughs and piled them on top of the Subject, creating a funeral pyre. He kept tossing branches onto the rising conflagration until an undulating wail of sirens from the village of Schierke below told him his time was up.

4

Each time before he set out to sea, Captain Edward Joseph Smith liked to walk his entire ship, stem to stern. It kept the men on their toes, if nothing else. And on this voyage, as much as and more than any other in his distinguished career, Captain Smith wanted his men on their toes. When *Titanic* launched in less than twenty-four hours, the whole world would be watching.

Activity on *Titanic* hummed at a fever pitch. He watched burly men, wet with sweat despite the cool April breeze coming off the water, labor to fill six holds with exotic cargo. Other workers craned aboard provisions—food and drink to satisfy more than two thousand paying passengers on a five-day voyage.

"To the left, you daft!" cried a red-faced able seaman at the crane operator, who was attempting to lower a cargo net containing a heavy wooden crate through the hatch coaming. The crane man scowled and spat.

"Doin' my best, aren't I?"

"We need a damn sight better than that," returned the seaman at the hatch. Then, with a start, he threw back his shoulders and broke into a full salute. The crane operator locked his controls and saluted as well. Neither man inhaled as the snow-bearded Captain

Smith, marching across the deck, stopped to glance quickly from net to crane. The captain scowled, and the seamen flinched. Had he heard them cursing and squabbling? Had they damaged the new hatch with their clumsy work? Finally, Smith nodded at the men and moved on.

"Thank you, Sir!" the seamen called after the captain in unison. Smith had read the situation immediately. The scowl was to end their fight and return focus to the job. After all, putting a little fear in the men kept them sharp.

Smith had put *Titanic* through her paces just days before, and the sea trials in Belfast had gone off satisfactorily. "She turns well enough, though damn slowly," Smith had remarked to *Titanic*'s designer, Mr. Thomas Andrews, who was aboard for the trials.

"I'm sure you've found that true of all large ships," said Andrews, not at all defensively. "And *Titanic* is larger than any." He was practically giddy. "From 12 knots to all-ahead-full speed in only ten minutes time," he enthused. "And when you called for a stop, she was still in the water less than a thousand yards after your order."

"Yes," allowed Smith. "She will serve."

Now, the Captain was eager to leave preparations behind and launch for America. There had been a lot of interest in the world's largest liner, and Smith had begrudgingly done his part to accommodate the press. "A sailor's best days at sea," he told one reporter, "are his first and his last." His last was close at hand. "All I want to do is put an oar on my shoulder and walk inland until someone asks what on earth that thing is. And that's where I'll spend the rest of my life."

For the better part of two decades, the sea had been his escape from everything he wished to leave behind on land. But as the years passed, the need for diversion had waned, and now he had a wife and daughter, Helen, waiting for him at the end of every voyage. How long until the girl was off having her own adventures? *Titanic*'s maiden trip across the Atlantic would be Smith's last at the helm of any ship. He was more than ready to hang up his captain's cap.

He had only one chore left to accomplish before sailing, and he trusted no man but himself to do it.

Captain Smith arrived at his suite, using a slim key to open the freshly painted white door. The three rooms were more luxurious than he needed, certainly more than he wanted. The parlor alone was the size of three steerage cabins. A polished chrome railing, its purpose more decorative than functional, circumnavigated the room. Four well-stuffed chairs surrounded a sophisticated mahogany table, upon which sat a long wooden crate that he'd delivered himself earlier that day.

Smith carefully lifted an oil painting from its nail. The still life depicted a bowl of figs. He'd have a steward find a more suitable spot for the work. It didn't belong in his cabin.

He reached inside a canvas sea bag and pulled out two wooden hooks, a small mallet, and a leather pouch containing a handful of mismatched screws and nails. He mounted the hooks in the holes where the painting had hung, cracking a little plaster along the way.

Using a pen knife, Captain Smith pried a brittle plank from atop the thin crate with a splintery pop. He removed a long, narrow package wrapped in midnight-blue silks, carefully unwinding the cloths to reveal a worn but rugged leather scabbard, with a loop for attaching to a belt. He kept the blade's slightly curved forty-four inches trapped safely inside the ceremonial sheath, with only a hammered brass pommel exposed to the air. In his hands, the treasure was curiously lightweight and substantial at the same time.

He carefully hung the sheathed sword on the hooks, then stepped back and admired his work. *Now stay up there on the wall where you belong*, Smith thought.

Captain Smith was ready to launch *Titanic*.

5

The rural British countryside flew past largely unseen, shrouded in darkness as the London and Southwest Railway train rumbled toward Southampton. A passenger car's paneled interior and its occupants were swallowed in shadow, intermittently illumined by shafts of moonlight darting through the windows. A lonely whistle blew, warning livestock of the approaching engine.

The Agent hadn't expected to be on a train in England. Instead of traveling to Russia, here he was trying to find that damn scientist, who'd blown up his laboratory and escaped with what Moltke had called "the Toxic." A thorough investigation of the Brocken Mountain facility had turned up an imposter vial, but no Theodor Weiss, alive or dead. Moltke was furious; so was the Kaiser. His order was to recover the Toxic and eliminate Weiss at all costs.

Yesterday evening, Weiss's Mercedes Simplex automobile had been discovered at Bremerhaven, and a man fitting his description had secured passage by steamer to Southampton. Weiss had fled to England, but would he remain there? Moltke was of the opinion the scientist would continue to America via *Titanic*. Its massive size made it the perfect ship in which to disappear.

Others felt differently, so Moltke had dispatched personnel to intercept Weiss at several potential destinations, but the Agent was determined to reach him first. He had requested the *Titanic* assignment, noting that if Germany couldn't apprehend Weiss before the ship sailed, they would need to make sure an operative was aboard. For the Agent, securing a false identity was paramount, and German intelligence had chosen the perfect candidate.

Reaching inside his rough, tweed jacket, the Agent withdrew a worn black-and-white photograph and referenced the picture one last time, using what light flittered in the car. The man in the picture had receding black hair combed straight back, tight to the scalp. Suspicious eyes were set close together, his dark, slanted eyebrows furrowed behind bowless, wire-rimmed spectacles. There was something of a mustache below his nose, though graying whiskers seemed to fade into his pallid face. He wore the uniform of a monarchist Russian: a coal-black top coat with a dark tie knotted high on his neck.

The Agent flipped the photo. The man's name was written on the back: Vitaly Jadovsky. Jadovsky would be traveling on *Titanic* alone, in first-class passage. He was ostensibly a newspaperman but in reality nothing more than a propagandist. According to the brief the Agent had memorized earlier during passage to England, Jadovsky's mission aboard *Titanic* was to reassure foreign investors that Russia was still a profitable place to do business, despite recent squabbles with labor.

His particulars were burned into the Agent's brain: Both father and mother died in a fire. Married to Ludmila, fourteen years. Three children. A fondness for Russian literature, Shutov vodka, and good tobacco. Jadovsky had acquired wealth by virtue of cheating two partners (including his own brother) of their rightful shares in a business venture. With his fortune and future secured, he'd concentrated for quite some time on writing inflammatory articles for the far right.

The Agent knew what kind of Russian Jadovsky was without ever meeting him.

The Agent stood and stretched, replacing the photograph in his pocket. It was time. He walked slowly down the aisle of the passenger car as if working out the kink in a trick knee that had stiffened on the journey. He passed Jadovsky, sitting alone and staring blankly out the window, and stopped two rows of seats behind him. The Agent then withdrew a pack of Sobranie cigarettes from his jacket and lit one. The smoke's red tip cast a bright glow as he inhaled, slowly and deeply.

The Russian noted the aroma at once, turning and smiling at the Agent. He gave Jadovsky a polite nod.

"Sobranie. Are you Russian?" asked Jadovsky in his native language.

"I am," replied the Agent without an accent. He produced the cigarette box again and offered one to Jadovsky. "Won't you join a countryman on the platform while I stretch my legs? I've been traveling on business for three days—the night air and company will do me good."

Jadovsky accepted the offer. He pulled on his long black coat and followed the Agent to the back of the car and through a sliding door.

The platform was considerably louder than inside the train car; the thunder of wheel meeting rail rattled up the men's legs and into their chests. The wooden floor shifted beneath them. High above, the nearly full moon glimmered between the tops of the cars, free of the city lights that dimmed its natural majesty.

The Agent handed Jadovsky the cigarette and lit it for him. The Russian closed his eyes and breathed in the fragrant smoke, holding it in his lungs for a full five seconds before exhaling. Bliss.

The Agent grinned and pulled on his own Sobranie, slowly releasing a trail of smoke into the cool night air. "What business are you in?" he asked.

"I'm a writer," replied Jadovsky.

"Interesting. What kind of things do you write?" asked the Agent.

"Editorials mostly."

"For whom?"

"*Russkoye Znamya.*"

"The Black Hundreds paper."

"That's right. Where are you from, friend?" Jadovsky asked, sticking out his hand.

The Agent grasped it tight. His eyes darkened. "Kishinev. I lived through the pogrom against the Jews. The pogrom your poisonous words incited."

Jadovsky blanched, his face stark with fear. He couldn't pull away from the Agent's cold, vice-like grip.

"Women raped; babies with their heads kicked in. My father, a toolmaker, killed with his own pliers. His blood pooled at my feet. The killers ceased to be human, and in exacting revenge, so shall I. Know this: once the last Jews depart Kishinev, I will destroy it."

With his free hand, the Agent reached into his jacket and pulled out a pair of needle-nose pliers, handcrafted by his dead father. The opened, pointed tips plunged into Jadovsky's neck, grabbed his Adam's apple, and jerked. Blood pumped from the fresh opening in time with the beating of the Russian's heart. Jadovsky slumped against the railing and opened his mouth to gasp, perhaps even to scream for help, but no sound came out.

The Agent had ripped his quarry's larynx free. A faint mist drifted up from where the hot wound met the crisp night air. He brought the tool down a second time, and a third, violent overhand blows to the dying man's chest, splintering his rib cage and puncturing both lungs. Reaching into Jadovsky's top coat, the Agent found a leather wallet containing a first-class *Titanic* ticket, a passport, and a small fortune in Russian currency.

Pocketing the credentials and ticket, he threw the money over the side of the train. Then he tucked the empty wallet back inside Jadovsky's coat, which he used to clean the pliers' silver prongs until they gleamed in the moonlight. The Agent carefully replaced the tool in his tweed jacket and lit another Sobranie. As he exhaled, he put a boot to the Russian's chest and kicked him hard over the railing into the darkness.

6

Weiss stumbled. His new cane and the broken cobbled streets of Southampton were not getting along. He was taking a circuitous route to the docks and watching for signs of being followed, but he'd seen nothing so far. He silently chastised himself for not adopting a better disguise than a set of ill-fitting traveling clothes and a three-day-old beard.

He rounded a corner and caught his first glimpse of the stacks. Four immense funnels loomed above the tops of the shipping offices and shops, casting shadows that stretched a good city block, like elongated fingers beckoning Southampton to explore the colossus lurking in her waters. Weiss picked up his pace. If these were the smokestacks, how big must the ship be?

Two blocks later, Weiss arrived before Dock Gate 4, Berth 34. He was thunderstruck by the sight of the mighty *Titanic* in its totality. It was as long as fifty automobiles and eight or nine stories high, which only took into account what bobbed above the waterline. Weiss had read a newspaper story that described the vessel's "nightmarish scale." Seeing it in person, he agreed: *Titanic* was truly a monster!

Weiss suddenly felt very small. He craned his neck up, stepping backward to fit *Titanic* into his field of vision. *Is this how the ant feels,* he wondered, *when faced with the enormity of a human?* He drew four breaths in the time it took his eyes to travel the length of the ship from pointed bow to massive stern. And what did God make of this creation of man?

Weiss pulled himself back into the present moment. He was no tourist. Anxiously, Weiss reached into the valise to again confirm the presence of his White Star boarding pass, the most important purchase he'd made during his short stay in Southampton. If he'd acquired a ticket by regular means, it would have been easy to trace his flight from Germany. He knew the ruse of his escape would not survive close scrutiny; the Kaiser's men were most likely calling at every port and transportation agent in Germany. But even if they discovered his first voyage to Southampton, there would be no paper trail of his second. The previous night, he had traversed the city asking about a *Titanic* berth for sale, till luck finally shined on him in a bawdy neighborhood pub. He'd procured a "Third Class (Steerage) Passenger's Contract Ticket" from a drunken fellow, who slurred, "I'm not going anywhere now! I've fallen in love, I have!" Weiss happily relieved Gregory P. Nosworthy of the burden of his ticket for seven pounds and a few pints of ale. He suspected a sober Nosworthy might be regretting his decision this very morning.

Weiss's second acquisition was his new wooden walking stick. Purchased in a filthy Southampton pawn shop not long after his transaction with Mr. Nosworthy, the cane was not what Weiss originally had in mind. He'd entered looking for a replacement pistol, one easily concealed inside a jacket. The shop's proprietor, Mr. Charles Lockerbie, was a gnarled old fellow in half-moon glasses working his way through a sorry apple.

"I need a gun," said Weiss upon entering.

"Hello to you," said Lockerbie and spit. "I'm fine and thank ye for asking."

"Forgive me," said Weiss awkwardly. "If it's not too much trouble, I'm looking for some personal protection in the form of a pistol. If you please."

"Nay, ye aren't," replied Lockerbie, bits of apple fighting to escape the corners of his mouth. "Shoot yourself in the foot, ye will, then yer wife will come back complainin' ta me."

Before Weiss could protest, Lockerbie crooked a finger at Weiss to follow him. He limped past carved tobacco pipes, silver pocket watches, and gaudy broaches. The old man wiped a hand wet with juice drippings on his vest, then produced a knotted walking stick from a brass stand. He tossed the staff to Weiss, who was surprised by its heft.

"You don't understand," Weiss protested. "I need protection—"

"Ack," interrupted Lockerbie, grabbing the cane back. He held the stick in one hand, grunting to get the German's attention, and tossed what was left of the apple on the floor. With a quick twist of the handle, a cruel six-inch blade sprung from the cane's end and locked into place with a satisfying metallic *thunk*. The old man stabbed the apple clean through and offered it to Weiss.

Weiss removed the apple and inspected the sturdy blade. In close quarters, a blade might prove more dependable than a pistol. He was not much of a shot, and guns could misfire. Hidden inside the cane, the knife was certainly more discreet. "Yes," he said, "this should do very nicely indeed."

Now Weiss leaned on his new stick as he surveyed the enormous crowd of passengers, gawkers, and well-wishers. Motor cars full of trunks honked their way through the assembly, while men in bowler hats checked their pocket watches and hurried to the proper gangways. Then with a start, and cursing his complacency, Weiss suddenly hurried to blend into the throngs of people. Tugging his cap down and shuffling toward the boarding lines, he thought, *I must remember to be more inconspicuous.*

7

The Agent stood atop a building overlooking the Southampton harbor. His perch was the perfect vantage point to watch a line of fidgeting third-class passengers boarding the ship. Gawkers clapped along with the band, competing with screeching gulls and the cheering crowd to create a boisterous din.

It had been seven years since the pogrom in Kishinev destroyed his life. He hated Weiss for delaying his revenge even one day longer. The wait would end today. The traitor hadn't shown himself as yet, but he would.

The Agent was confident he could spot Theodor Weiss in the black of night during a thunderstorm, and on this morning, the bright sun shone in a clear blue sky. Weiss would travel as a third-class passenger: scientists were logical to a fault. To disappear, he'd pick the most unassuming form of passage. Weiss was among this crowd; of that, the Agent was certain.

No one who knew the real Vitaly Jadovsky would mistake the Agent for the propagandist, but a bit of disguise went a long way. The Agent was now a fair match for the Russian's grainy passport photo. Dressed in a black top coat with black tie and gray whiskers (attached to his chin with spirit gum), he should easily pass through customs. Then again, perhaps he wouldn't need to . . .

For there was Weiss!

The Agent established the vial's hiding place instantly—in the worn black satchel the scientist clutched tightly in his left hand. Even from the rooftop, the Agent could see the tension in Weiss's fist and forearm.

The Agent swiftly made his way to street level and entered the moving current of the crowd, keeping Weiss in his sights. The scientist was clearly traveling alone, with no companion to call for help or play the hero. Perfect. The raucous mob scene provided sufficient cover, but also a logistical problem: How to snatch the bag with the least fuss and fewest witnesses?

Closing in on his target, the Agent quickly considered his options. Killing Weiss was best, but it was unlikely to go unnoticed or unchallenged in such a crowd. It was also risky to murder the defector before the Agent was certain he had the Toxic. After the ruse with the dummy vial on Brocken Mountain, the Agent could not dismiss the possibility that Weiss might pull the trick again. The simplest ploy was to knock down Weiss from behind, then grab the bag in the confusion and quickly disappear into the masses. If the Agent couldn't steal and authenticate the Toxic before the ship sailed, he'd finish his business on board.

A steam whistle let out a blast. His whole body went taut. He was within thirty feet of Weiss—only to be brought to a dead stop by an unacceptable development.

"Boy."

Weiss beckoned to a scruffy youth standing alone on the dock, peering up at *Titanic*'s imposing stacks from beneath an oversized newsboy's cap. The child's hands were stuffed inside a dingy, charcoal-colored coat that was too large by a third. Only scuffed leather boots were visible beneath the worn black cloth.

"Who are you calling 'boy'?"

Weiss held out a few dull coins in the palm of his hand. "You, if it's not too much bother. I'm offering a paying job. It's simple enough, unless you have no use for money?"

The child's face brightened a bit. "Call me Lou."

The youth approached Weiss tentatively, the way a squirrel might creep toward an old man offering a handful of nuts. Lou appeared to be no more than eleven years old, perhaps twelve, with locks of rust-colored hair attempting to escape the confines of the cap. A patch of skin missing from his nose indicated a spill or a fight. The scrape suited him, either way.

Weiss eased the urchin a few coins. "Just stand here and talk to me." *And anyone searching the crowd will expect me to be alone,* he thought, *not traveling with a child.* "My stomach is feeling a little unsettled. I'll gladly pay for a little conversation. It would be a welcome distraction."

"Seasick already? We're not even on the boat!" The boy examined the coins—they appeared genuine. With a shrug, he cleaned his right hand against his cloth coat and offered it to Weiss. "Lou Goodwin. Good to know you."

"Hello, Lou," said Weiss. "I'm G. P. Nosworthy."

"It's a pleasure, G. P."

"That's Mr. Nosworthy to you."

Lou arched an eyebrow. "High class, I get it. A real Guggenheim."

Weiss stared blankly. "A real Googen . . . ?"

Lou pointed to a parade of first-class passengers making their way across a gangplank six stories up. "Guggenheim," the kid said, noting a gentleman in an expensive straw hat. "He's the one with the hundred-pound mustache."

Weiss frowned. "How do you know that's Mr. Guggenheim?"

"He's the Sultan of Smelt!" cried Lou. "Worth millions! Don't you read the papers?"

"I generally don't find gossip and scandal worth reading," said Weiss.

"Whatever you say, mister. But I'll tell you this: I sell fifty copies before noon most days. With good gossip, seventy-five." Lou sized up the strange gentleman with the odd accent. "What are you in, anyway?"

"Exports," the German replied.

Judging by Weiss's rather ordinary clothing, Lou decided there must not be much money in exports.

Weiss was now only ten or twelve people away from the ticket takers. He looked around furtively for signs of anyone following him. All seemed ordinary. He was nearly on the ship, mere steps away from escape.

"Oh! There's one for you," said Lou. "That's the Lady Cardeza. 'Lady' because she used to be married to a Spanish king or duke or some sort. Watched them unload her automobile this morning—how many trunks you wager she's bringing on board?"

"I couldn't speculate," said Weiss, becoming distracted as the line trickled forward.

"Would it kill you to make a guess?" asked Lou. "You're payin' for this. *Fourteen* trunks! Enough to fill two houses. All that money and she can't even keep her hair on straight."

Weiss drew his attention to the matron in a polar bear fur coat, slowly making her way into first-class passage. As Lou had observed, Lady Cardeza's silver-blue hair was traveling southward into her eyes.

"Spend some of that dough on a hair pin, why don't ya!" shouted Lou. A firm hand grabbed Lou's ear and spun the child round.

"I've been looking for you for nearly an hour!" scolded a serious young woman wearing a fancy ruffled hat that didn't quite match her dress. "Have you lost your mind, Louise?"

"Louise?" Weiss exclaimed. He took a second look at the waif. Sure enough, it was a girl hidden beneath the oversized cap. *Since when are girls allowed to sell newspapers?* Weiss thought.

Lou twisted to escape the tight grip on her ear, but it was no use. She pleaded to Weiss, "Been here all along, haven't I, mister?"

The woman noticed Weiss for the first time. She released Lou's ear, straightened up, and smoothed her dress with her gloved hands. "Has my daughter been bothering you? She was meant to be back at the hotel changing clothes for the journey."

"Told you, it's too cold for that frilly thing," said Lou, crossing her arms defiantly.

"No," replied Weiss, clearing his throat. "Not bothering me at all." The woman's pretty blue eyes still sparked with anger behind perfectly round spectacles. "I must say, she seems to know a great deal about the world."

"Not half as much as she believes," said the woman. "I'm sorry for the trouble." She allowed a small smile and firmly took Lou's hand. "Come on now. Don't get lost before we can even get to America."

"I assure you, there was no trouble," Weiss said, remembering to tip his cap. "A pleasant journey to you."

The young woman acknowledged his courtesy with a polite nod, then yanked Lou's arm as she turned away. The girl waved back, grinning broadly. "Did you hear that, mister? We're going to America!"

9

Taking a moment away from his crew on the bridge, Captain Edward J. Smith crossed callused hands over his broad chest and exhaled. *Titanic* wasn't even an hour into her maiden voyage, and already she nearly had suffered a collision. He had hoped for a less dramatic onset to the journey.

It wasn't that he believed everything always went according to plan. Quite the opposite. His experience facing the unexpected was what made him such an effective sea captain. Since *Titanic*'s maiden voyage would also be Smith's last, he was even more on guard than usual.

All had looked well as *Titanic* prepared for launch. It glided out of the Southampton berth easy as you please and out toward sea. Cheering onlookers ran along the docks, chasing *Titanic*. Two additional ships moored in the harbor, *New York* and *Oceanic*, were full of passengers who had paid a fine price, not to sail, but for a deckside view of the world's largest liner as it embarked for the first time.

The trouble began as *Titanic* passed the two smaller ships. Even at a slow launch speed, *Titanic*'s massive triple-screw propellers created a mighty churn. The wake created by its twenty-six-thousand-ton hull was so powerful that the sturdy ropes tethering *New York* and *Oceanic* to the docks strained tight. Then, *New York*'s ropes snapped loudly enough to be mistaken for shotguns firing, and the ship was slowly sucked toward the side of *Titanic*.

Smith had experienced a similar calamitous scenario only seven months prior. That time, a small warship got caught in the wake of Smith's *Olympic*. The smaller vessel was dragged into the liner, ripping a serious wound in the larger boat's side. Smith wasn't blamed—the docks and harbors simply couldn't accommodate the new breed of giant liners. "Too big to handle!" proclaimed the naysayers.

Smith believed otherwise. With *New York* dangerously close to ramming *Titanic*, he stood tall in his ceremonial dress whites and calmly ordered *Titanic*'s port propeller into high gear. The ensuing wash pushed the smaller boat away, and *Titanic* came to a virtual halt, avoiding impact by a matter of feet.

There was a fair amount of whooping and back-slapping among the men in the wheelhouse, but Smith put a stop to it. "Back to your posts," he commanded. "Celebrate on your leave. There's still work to be done."

In the Café Parisien, a luxury saloon for *Titanic*'s first-class passengers, chatter filled the air. To be sure, between the cheering crowds and the band's merry playing, most of the travelers had no inkling there had been any danger. Yet several prominent passengers witnessed the near-miss, and J. Bruce Ismay, chairman and managing director of the White Star Line, felt his ears burn at the whispers:

Is she safe?

Off to a poor start, I'd say!

Bad omen!

Ismay knew it was a habit of the rich to find fault. His marriage to a society girl ensured he never forgot. Quibbling over the color of the cabin walls and the quality of the cutlery—all to be expected. But was it too much to ask that Smith get *Titanic* out of harbor without incident?

"All's well, Bruce?"

George Dunton Widener, a solidly built man with rimless, nose-pinch spectacles and a waxed moustache, slapped a beefy hand on Ismay's shoulder. Ismay was a taller man than most, but Widener, a board member of the Philadelphia bank that controlled White Star Line, could still make him feel like a boy.

"Quite well, as you can see," replied Ismay. "Why, we'll be in Cherbourg before you can whistle 'Alexander's Ragtime Band.'"

"Very good," laughed Widener, lighting a cigar and blowing smoke into the lounge's ornate fixtures. "We have seven and a half million reasons to wish for a successful voyage, you and me."

Ismay managed a humorless smile. He knew full well the cost of building *Titanic* and how much White Star's fleet was mortgaged to pay for her. He wasn't about to give Widener the satisfaction of seeing him perspire.

"To celebrate our successful launch," Ismay announced with a grand wave of his hand, "our best champagne for everyone!"

The stewards set corks flying into the air, and Ismay let the applause of *Titanic*'s wealthy wash away his distress. Perhaps the worst was over. That was the best way to look at it. Ismay wasn't going to let anything tarnish the glory of his triumph.

10

Weiss found his way down *Titanic*'s winding stairs and narrow hall-ways. Brass railings gleamed, marred only by their first fingerprints. The cream-colored walls appeared still wet with fresh paint.

If anything, the ship seemed even bigger on the inside, and its confusing layout didn't help matters. Once below, passengers couldn't travel directly from the ship's front to back—bulkheads bisected the decks at odd intervals, necessitating trips down flights of stairs, through corridors, and then back up again. He'd expected the passengers to be separated on different decks by class, but that wasn't exactly the case. While first-class accommodations were generally on the upper levels, they sometimes neighbored second-class cabins, which were found on all seven passenger decks. Eventually, Weiss stopped trying to make sense of the layout, winding his way through the maze of second- and third-class cabins on Deck E until he found Cabin 156 toward the back of the ship.

His ticket demanded that he share the room and its two sets of polished wooden bunks with three other men. The cabin had space for little else. Weiss arrived first and claimed a bottom berth; a proper spring mattress and feather pillows to boot were more than he had expected. He was used to scratchy military-issue bedding that smelled as if it had been boiled in bleach.

Eventually, his cabin-mates appeared: two down-on-their-luck Bulgarian brothers and a moody Finn—not Weiss's preferred company, but a suitable group to disappear in for a few days. He eyed them for signs of disease common to steerage folk: typhoid, typhus, cholera. They appeared healthy enough. Weiss grimaced when he realized there was only one shared bathing tub for all the third-class men. The room's smell promised to ripen. He aimed to spend as little time in quarters as possible.

Weiss allowed himself a moment of relief and wondered: Had he truly escaped? Except for the fare-thee-well commotion and celebration, boarding the *Titanic* had been uneventful, more than he'd dared hope. He was proud of his deception with the girl, Louise, but perhaps now that he was safely aboard, more subterfuge wouldn't be necessary. He could begin planning his next step. The crossing gave him five nights to consider his future in America.

But such thoughts could wait. What he needed now was a steaming cup of Earl Grey tea. His only luggage was his valise, and for a brief second he considered leaving it locked in the room when he ventured out. Then he immediately cursed himself for a fool. Perhaps he'd escaped his pursuers, but did he think *Titanic* lacked garden-variety thieves? The bag's contents were too important to leave unattended, and his cabin-mates looked just the types to rummage a man's things if given the chance. His cane would also need to be a constant companion. In fact, it would not be a bad idea to sleep with it at his side.

Weiss wandered into the third-class general room in search of refreshment and found that seemingly every other passenger in steerage had the same idea. The pine-paneled common area, trimmed in gleaming white enamel, teemed with passengers thrilled to be at sea.

Weiss settled himself into an empty spot on a smooth teak bench, secured his valise between his shoes, and took in the frenzied surroundings. Men filled their pipes and spun tales. Children chased one another; clucking mothers ran after them. A bagpipe player sat in the corner, playing woeful tunes. The bleating music competed with the sound of boisterous conversation.

"Mr. Nosworthy?"

Weiss didn't respond, lost in all the activity and noise.

"Mr. Nosworthy? Anyone sitting here?"

Weiss looked up to find a girl fidgeting in a dark wool skirt and ruffled shirt, threadbare in places but clean. *Of course, Lou, the child from the dock.* Apparently, her mother had won the wardrobe argument, and the girl didn't look to like it one bit. Her copper hair fought against the bow her mother had tied, and mad curls struggled to break free as Lou impatiently shifted her weight from one foot to the other. Something about the girl's piercing gaze reminded Weiss very much of his sister, Sabine, and he felt a shock of recognition. It was a look he hadn't seen in twenty years.

The bench was full of passengers, but Weiss shifted to create a space beside him. "By all means."

Lou squeezed herself in, all elbows and knees, defiantly unladylike. "Where's your family?" she asked bluntly. "Don't you have a wife?"

"I don't, actually." Weiss coughed and adjusted his collar. He was uncomfortable with personal questions, even when he wasn't traveling incognito. "Not that it's any of your business."

"That's too bad," Lou said, raising her eyebrows and swinging her legs beneath the bench. "My mum ain't married neither, not since Papa died. That's why we're headed to Iowa City."

Weiss cleared his throat again. "I'm sorry to hear about your father."

"Wasn't around much anyways," said Lou. "He liked ramblin'."

Weiss nodded. Still swinging her legs, Lou continued, "Mum's brother George is a professor at a school in Iowa City. I'm going to study frogs. Once we save some money."

"A scientist, eh?" Weiss said with approval. "They allow girls to be scientists in Iowa?"

Lou's eyes narrowed. "The best scientists in Iowa are women."

"I'm sure they are," Weiss chuckled. He shifted the valise between his shoes. "What happened to your nose?"

"Ugly pug two blocks over tried to sell papers on my corner," said Lou. She held up a fist. "Had to set the bum straight."

Weiss shifted. "I see. Does your mother approve of the way you settled that dispute, Lou?"

The girl grinned broadly, wrinkling her nose. "Nope, but I did tell him to scram first. He said no and started calling me names. I cussed him right back—I can cuss and swear with the best of 'em!—but I could see it was no use." She shrugged proudly. "This little scrape ain't nothing compared to what I gave . . ."

"Louise!"

The girl's mother stormed toward them, her auburn hair now free of her frilly hat. The other passengers on the bench leaned away, wanting no part of her anger. "You promised—no more talking to strangers!" she cried. She flushed as she turned to Weiss. "Begging your pardon again, sir."

"Mr. Nosworthy isn't a stranger," protested Lou. "We've been properly introduced."

Weiss held up his palms.

Lou said to her mother, "Don't you think you should invite him to eat with us? That's good manners, ain't it?"

Weiss turned red and stammered. He didn't want Mrs. Goodwin to think he had any ulterior motives. "Really, I . . . I . . ."

"I'm sure the gentleman has other plans," said Mrs. Goodwin, taking Lou by the arm and pulling her forcefully off the bench. "She won't be bothering you again, you have my word."

"It's no bother," he said, but mother and daughter were already moving away and didn't hear.

"He has to eat," Lou grumbled as her mother pulled her away.

11

"Let us drink to the mighty *Titanic*!"

Passengers in the world's largest floating room erupted in cheers of approval, and many stood to raise their glasses. With a sweep of his arm, Dr. William O'Loughlin hoisted his tumbler to the assembled and enjoyed a healthy swig of rye before retaking his seat at the captain's table. His cheeks flushed warm, both from the applause and the drink.

In a corner of the room, Wallace Hartley launched the *Titanic* band into a lilting waltz, the violins' melody line lifting above the applause. Leading this group marked the pinnacle of Hartley's career, and his pride showed in the flourish of his bow. He smiled and winked at O'Loughlin as the man took his seat.

O'Loughlin sat, as usual, with his good friend, the architect Thomas Andrews. Boyish and thrilled to finally be at sea on *Titanic* after years spent dreaming her into existence, Andrews slapped the doctor on the back good-naturedly. "Perhaps you should skip the toasts and stick to curing the sick," Andrews laughed.

The captain's table was small, seating only six, but it was still the most prominent table in the first-class dining saloon, positioned forward and center of the rest. O'Loughlin and Andrews were joined by

Lady Cardeza and her companion for the evening, businessman Emil
Kaufmann, J. Bruce Ismay, and, of course, Captain Smith himself. A
succulent smell of roast duckling filled the room. Now that *Titanic*
was well out to sea, good spirits abounded.

"You'll forgive me," said Ismay to the Lady Cardeza, "if I celebrate
too much this evening? Many years of hard work bear fruit tonight!"

"You'll only be forgiven," smiled the Lady Cardeza, motioning lan-
guidly for a steward carrying a bottle of red wine, "if you allow us to
join the celebration." Mr. Kaufmann bent his brow to the steward—a
gesture meant to communicate, "She's had enough, thank you."

Ismay took in the room yet again, with its leaded windows and
Jacobean-style alcoves. There had to be ten millionaires—millionaires!—in this saloon alone. "My God," he said. "*Titanic* puts *Lusita-
nia* to shame. Larger by half. And grander beyond measure."

Mr. Kaufmann stifled a laugh into his napkin. Lady Cardeza
joined in the laughter as well, but at what she would have been hard
pressed to say.

"Do you find something funny, sir?" Ismay asked.

"Not at all," replied Kaufmann dryly. "She's a beautiful ship. *Grand*
is just the word."

"I haven't told you nearly enough about my new friend, Mr.
Kaufmann," said Lady Cardeza. "He claims to be unattached, which
I find hard to believe. And did I mention Emil is also in the shipping
business? You two have so much in common!"

"You didn't mention," said Ismay. "What line, if I may ask?"

"Hamburg Amerika," said Kaufmann.

Ismay bristled—no doubt Kaufmann was aboard on a fact-finding
mission. The German line's *Deutschland* had won the Blue Riband for
fastest passenger liner to cross the Atlantic. *Titanic* would certainly
pose a threat to that. "Funny," said Ismay. "I thought I knew every
man of consequence at Hamburg Amerika."

"I'm new," Kaufmann replied without elaboration.

There was an uncomfortable silence at the table as Ismay sized up the German, a big man with nondescript features. Ismay disliked Kaufmann immediately. Lady Cardeza, feeling silences were meant to be broken, raised her refilled glass for another toast.

"To *Titanic!*" she said. "May she sail a thousand voyages!"

"I designed her to sail *ten thousand*," Ismay said pointedly, "come hell or high water."

Andrews shifted in his seat and grinned, while Kaufmann let loose with a hearty "Hear, hear!" Andrews was happy to let Mr. Ismay have the spotlight. For Andrews, *Titanic*'s successful launch was reward enough. Not that work on the ship was finished. He kept a small notebook with him at all times to jot down any imperfections he observed or ideas for improvement. For example, he already wished he'd fought harder for the glass dome that would have served as this room's ceiling.

"Let's not tempt the fates," said Captain Smith. "I'd prefer to leave the devil out of this."

Ismay grimaced. Smith's relentless sobriety was spoiling both Ismay's mood and his moment of triumph. "You know how special this ship is, Captain," Ismay said. "But perhaps Mr. Andrews can explain to our guests why *Titanic* is unique and unrivaled?" Asking Andrews to speak about *Titanic* was like asking a mother about her child. Andrews's enthusiasm for his prodigy carried them right through to the end of their meal.

"Fifteen bulkheads rise from the bottom of the ship—some as far up as Deck E!—essentially creating sixteen individual compartments. Each compartment is watertight, or at least it is once we close the special doors."

Kaufmann sniffed. "Yes, but it would be difficult to do by hand in an emergency—"

"Exactly!" Andrews interrupted. "That's why we designed a new type of system. If, God forbid, the ship took on water from any sort of collision, we can close all the doors from the bridge via electronic switch."

"Electronics!" exclaimed Lady Cardeza.

"Electronics that trigger hydraulically operated, vertically sliding doors, a design exclusive to Harland and Wolff," Andrews explained with pride. "Why, even if *Titanic* took on water in *four* of those compartments, she would still stay afloat and sail on to her destination!"

"Unsinkable!" Ismay pounded the table and leaned at Kaufmann. "*Shipbuilder* magazine itself said so!"

"You don't seem so sure, E. J.," Lady Cardeza cooed to the captain, casually adjusting her hair. "I don't know how to swim. Is *Titanic* truly unsinkable?"

"I cannot imagine any condition," said Smith, "that would cause this good ship to founder. Thanks to men like Mr. Andrews, modern shipbuilding has gone beyond that."

Andrews's ears went red from the compliment. He grinned and pushed food around his plate.

"Then you agree with my assessment," said Ismay, satisfied that he'd bested Kaufmann. "*Titanic* represents man's triumph over the sea!"

Lady Cardeza took another swig of wine and leaned into the table. "But is it true what they say," she said in a loud stage whisper, "about the ghost?"

Ismay coughed into his fist. "I have no idea what you're talking about."

"One of the porters whispered it to me earlier," said Lady Cardeza. "He said *Titanic* is haunted by a man who was trapped inside the walls of the ship itself! Is it true? I can't imagine anything so *horrible*."

Captain Smith clipped a long cigar and fired its end. A cerulean trail of smoke drifted toward the ceiling. "Go on. Tell her about our ghost, Mr. Andrews."

"Yes, please do, Thomas," said O'Loughlin.

"Fairy tales," Ismay scoffed.

"Oh please," urged Lady Cardeza, "you can tell me. I won't breathe a word of it to anyone."

"If it's all right, Mr. Ismay," said Andrews, "I'll tell the tale. Sensible people will recognize the story for what it is."

Lady Cardeza clapped her hands in delight. Kaufmann grinned as well. Mr. Ismay did not raise further protest.

"The gossip began," Andrews said, "when a shipyard worker supposedly slipped and fell unnoticed into the steel hull. Some say his name was Wassell. Others say Sclater."

"Yes, but what *was* his name?" asked Lady Cardeza.

"He doesn't have a name because he doesn't exist. But as the story goes, our mystery man was knocked unconscious, and his coworkers, unaware of his presence inside the hull, entombed the man inside. At night—" Here Andrews paused for dramatic effect. "—the shipyard men say that you can still hear the poor sod pounding the walls of his prison, trying to alert the world to his horrific fate."

"I heard knocking this very evening," exclaimed Lady Cardeza, eyes wide.

"No doubt the steward with his corkscrew," said O'Loughlin with a chuckle. Lady Cardeza harrumphed.

"There are a hundred such stories for every ship that's built," said Andrews. "I thought I could dispel this one by conducting a full investigation. Nothing and no one was ever found. But by refusing to ignore the gossip, I seem to have only given it stronger legs."

"Rumor and innuendo have torn down far more than they have ever built," said Ismay, shaking his head.

"I did turn the tale to my advantage, however," said Andrews with a wry grin. "I took to calling the hull 'the Tomb' as a way to remind the men their work was dangerous. And that did it, by God. Injuries went down more than 15 percent."

"Well played," said Kaufmann, as if conceding a point.

"And there you are," Ismay said. "Another example of modern man overcoming superstition. We have entered an age in which men of science and industry can bend the world to their will."

"So it would seem, Mr. Ismay," said Captain Smith. "Still, I believe it's wise to maintain a healthy respect of the unknown."

"Oh, please, Captain. Don't tell me *you* have more horror stories to share!" chided Ismay.

"Some stories," replied Smith, "are not meant for the dinner table."

Ismay regarded the captain. "That reminds me of some fine advice from Robert Louis Stevenson: *Keep your fears to yourself and share your courage with others.*"

"Wise words," agreed Smith. "Reminds me of another saying I picked up during my time in Arabia, though I don't know who said it first."

"What is it?" implored the Lady Cardeza. The others leaned in as well.

"*Arrogance,*" said Smith, "*diminishes wisdom.*"

12

By the morning of *Titanic*'s second full day at sea, Theodor Weiss no longer felt the rush of his escape. The events seemed dreamlike now, with his arms against the railing, a full stomach from breakfast, and the endless ocean reaching to the horizon.

But Weiss still felt unsettled. The burden of the Toxic weighed on him more heavily than Lady Cardeza's fourteen trunks. All his thoughts had bent toward escape. He'd given little consideration to what he would do once he reached America. First, he needed to set up a fully-equipped laboratory. That required funding, and his own accounts were insufficient, if he could even access them now. There was security to consider as well. A military facility was in some respects ideal, but he no longer trusted any government. Would America really act any differently than Germany? Perhaps a wealthy patron could provide support. He had no family to lean on.

If only his sister, Sabine, were still alive. As a boy, he thought that having a twin of the opposite gender was strange. "She doesn't even look like me," he would object, though everyone else thought they looked startlingly similar. His boyish protests reminded him of Louise. "Her hair is so long and wild!"

But their hearts and minds were joined, and young Theodor knew it, regardless of what he said to save face with others. The twins could not lie to each other—even when parents and other adults swallowed the children's fabrications whole, Sabine and Theodor could tell when the other was casting falsehoods. Yet it cut even deeper than that. When Sabine's feelings were bruised, some part of him felt her pain.

He thought of the tree they used to scale as children, a Norway spruce with plenty of low branches. In the summer, the tree's bark seeped with sap—quite a chore to scrub off later, but the sticky gum offered a reassuring tackiness that made Theodor feel as if he couldn't fall, like a spider defying gravity.

But the spruce still offered trials, most notably a gap about three meters off the ground, between sets of sturdy branches. Sabine was the stronger climber, and she would shimmy up the fat trunk to reach the next big limb, then swing her legs until she somehow ended up in a sitting position above him, grinning like a cat.

"You can do it, Theodor!" she'd holler.

But he couldn't, not like her. He'd stare up helplessly, until finally she would take pity on him and reach down to grab his wrist. With her strong right arm pulling him up, he could grab hold of the next branch and scramble up next to her. That was what she was for him, the little boost that made all the difference. After catching their breath, they'd keep climbing higher together in the bright afternoon sun.

The glint off the ocean spray brought Weiss back to the present moment. He tightened his grip on the valise handle. Whenever he felt challenged, he often imagined holding out his arm for Sabine. Whatever the problem was, the thought of her always helped pull him through. Now, he would keep his promise to her. He would find a cure for the plague that killed her.

Weiss returned to the common room to shake off the cold of wind and sea. He found a place on a bench, securing the valise on his lap and leaning his walking stick against an arm rest. The room was quieter in the morning, which was more to his liking.

"Mr. Nosworthy?"

A steward touched Weiss's shoulder and handed him a small enve-lope addressed in a childish script, rendered in thick pencil. *Louise*, he thought.

Weiss unsealed the envelope and withdrew the *Titanic* stationery card, emblazoned with a red flag marked by a single white star. He struggled to read the juvenile scribble:

> *Mr. Nosworthy my mum did not come back to our cabin*
> *last night and I'm worried something awful. I want to go*
> *look for her but don't want to leave on my own. Can you*
> *help? I'm scared. Please come see me. Lou, cabin F2*

Frowning, Weiss folded the note in quarters and shoved it inside his breast jacket pocket. Was the girl in real distress or only match-making? Surely, alerting a crewmember was the best way to find her lost mother. In all likelihood, she had found some other gentleman more to her liking last night and would return to her cabin at any moment. As endearing as Lou was, Weiss didn't have time to get entangled in her family troubles. *If everyone just kept to themselves*, thought Weiss, *the world would be a much better place.* Yet he couldn't just ignore Lou's request. His conscience dictated that he go and help her, if she still needed it. Then he could put an end to their acquaintance.

The scientist grabbed his valise and cane and made his way down three sets of orange-lit staircases to Deck F. Down in steerage, he could feel the rumble of the ship's massive turbines in his feet. The grumbling sound grew louder as the room numbers on the lacquered white doors became progressively smaller: F40, F32, F16.

He turned the corner and rapped loudly on the door to F2. Weiss knocked again, but still no one answered. Had Lou now run off?

There were no sounds of footsteps inside, though it was hard to hear over the turbine engines. Weiss reached inside his jacket to confirm the room number in Lou's note when something heavy struck him in the back of the head. His legs went out beneath him, and as he was dragged down the corridor, he lost consciousness.

When Weiss came to, he was tied securely to a chair, unable to move. His hands and feet were bound, and more cords wrapped around his chest. A pillowcase covered his head, making it hard to breathe and impossible to see.

How long had he been out? Like an electric shock, Weiss remembered his valise and shouted through the linen: "Where am I? What do you want? Where's the girl? If it's money you want, take what I have, but you chose the wrong fellow!"

A man chuckled. A bulky shadow passed in front of the ceiling light. Weiss's labored breathing was hot and moist against the cloth.

"Perhaps you should have accepted the girl's dinner invitation," the stranger said.

Weiss silently cursed himself. Had he fallen for a con? Had Lou played him for a fool, and for what? A few coins?

"Did you enlist her in this?" Weiss asked, hoping the answer was "no."

The man laughed. "Hardly, but I *should* pay her. On a vessel this size, I might have spent half the journey looking for you, but the idea of her in trouble led you right to me."

"Damn it, what do you want?" Weiss shouted.

The man's voice dropped to a whisper, close by Weiss's ear. "I think you know, Herr Theodor Weiss. Tell me, how is your research progressing? It's a shame about your facility in the Harz Mountains. Burnt to ashes. Such a terrible *accident*."

Weiss froze. The man moved away, retrieving something from behind him.

The scientist heard his bag being opened. A muted Russian accent crept into the man's voice. "It's like a nesting doll, yes? Inside the bag, there is a steel container." Weiss heard the sound of the container twisting open. "And inside the container, a vial. And inside the vial . . ."

"Who are you?" demanded Weiss. "The Kaiser's agent?"

"If you like. Let's say I'm the man who will take what you've stolen. The man who will kill you."

"That vial is a fake!" Weiss shouted in desperation. "I have hidden the real one. You'll never find it!"

"You did try to fool us once with a counterfeit, Herr Weiss," the Agent growled, "and it's plausible that you would do so again. I suppose there's only way to know for certain."

Weiss flinched as the Agent lifted the pillowcase just enough to expose Weiss's mouth. A hand pressed against the scientist's forehead, pushing it back.

"What do you say, Herr Weiss? Shall we make a monster?"

"The vial contains cyanide," said Weiss quickly.

"Come, you can do better than that."

"I'd rather die than see the Toxic used as a weapon. I knew I would be pursued, and that I might have to kill myself to protect my secrets. Feed me the fluid, but know that when I'm dead, the true location of the Toxic perishes with me."

For a long moment, the attacker neither moved nor spoke. The only sound was the rumbling turbines powering *Titanic* west. Then all at once, the Agent released his grip on Weiss, speaking calmly and pacing in front of him. "Yes, it is a risk. All's lost for me if this were to kill you rather than infect you. But are you actually that noble, to die rather than turn over the weapon? You seem the type. Then again, perhaps you are merely a good actor."

The Agent stopped pacing. "Another thing puzzles me: If you're so intent on the Toxic not being used as a weapon, why did you not destroy it on Brocken Mountain?"

"I will use it to find a cure for the plague!" Weiss shouted. "No one deserves such horror!"

"I know who deserves it!" The man's hand closed around Weiss's throat and squeezed ferociously, cutting off his windpipe until pinpoints of light sparkled in the darkness behind his eyelids. "And I'm going to give it to them."

The Agent released Weiss, who choked and gasped. He heard the sound of the vial sliding back inside the steel cylinder and its lid being screwed back on.

"The Toxic—or the cyanide—will now be tested on an innocent. Know that you have sentenced him to die."

"No! Dear God, don't do that!"

"Enough talk, Herr Weiss!" The pillowcase was raised again, and the Agent's hand, cool and strong, gripped Weiss's jaw. "Understand. No one escapes my punishment."

A pointed metal object forced its way into Weiss's mouth. He desperately clenched his jaw against the unforgiving metal, but the effort was futile. The pliers dug farther in, cutting his tongue and latching onto one of his left bottom molars. Weiss thrashed as it was wrenched side to side with excruciating brutality. After three sickening *cracks,* the tooth gave way and was jerked from his mouth.

Before Weiss could scream, the man gagged him with fresh linen. Weiss choked hard and felt blood force its way out his nose. The gag quickly saturated with blood. Unbearable pain roared inside his mouth, making thought impossible. He heard his tooth skitter across the floor.

A door opened and Weiss lifted his head in agony. Through the cloth, he saw the Agent's imposing silhouette framed in a rectangle of light.

"When I return, Herr Weiss, it won't be a tooth my pliers pull next. There are many ways they can kill a man."

Weiss heard the door close before he lost consciousness.

13

Weiss came to, overwhelmed by pain. He could not say how long he had been out.

Eventually, Weiss managed to regain some control of his faculties as the most intense spikes of pain receded to a throbbing, pulsating ache. He shook the pillowcase free from his head and blinked, disoriented, surrounded by stacks of white: a linen closet, not Lou's cabin. He tugged uselessly at his bindings and swallowed blood, which still flowed from the empty socket and his lacerated gums.

Weiss forced long, slow breaths through his nose till eventually he became calm enough to put a coherent thought together. He had to get free.

The Kaiser's agent was testing the Toxic. But if Weiss could get free, he could at least warn others, the ship's doctors, *the captain*. They could help him quarantine any infected, then find the man who stole the vial. Yes, if they could do that, maybe it would be all right. All was not lost yet.

How long has he been gone? wondered Weiss. *No matter. If I'm still here when that man comes back, I'm dead.*

First, he had to get rid of the gag in his mouth. It kept him from spitting, and the accumulated blood in his stomach was making him sick. Eventually he would vomit. Some of the discharge might escape out his nose, but the rest would be forced back into his lungs. The gag would cause him to drown *aboard* the *Titanic*.

Fighting off a surge of fear, he focused on his surroundings. A shelf on his far right held linens and bottles of laundry agents. They were no help. The left held no more promise, dominated by stacks of pillowcases and bed sheets. His valise was nowhere to be seen. He stomped his feet in frustration.

The motion rocked his chair backward, and it teetered, precariously close to tipping over. Weiss quickly thrust forward, causing the seat to swing in that direction. Even though his feet were bound together, he got his legs under him enough to set the seat firmly back on the floor. The episode gave him an idea.

Using the same motion, he jumped the chair off the ground and spun it sideways. The back of the room held more stacks of linens, but in the far right corner he saw something familiar. His cane lay just in front of a shelving unit atop two bags of dirty sheets. Weiss shimmied the chair toward the stick.

He positioned himself so that a shelf was in front of him and his cane behind him. He estimated the distance, adjusted again, and after two calming breaths, leaned back. Locking his toes under the shelf, he felt for the cane with his bound hands. His fingertips found it just as his feet slipped, pulling the shelf toward him.

As the shelf slowly began to topple, he grasped wildly for the cane until it was in his hands, then he threw his shoulder forward and slammed into the falling shelf. It fell back against the wall with a heavy bounce. He had done it.

Weiss twisted the handle and activated the blade, then he slid the cane until the blade was behind the ropes that bound his wrists. The blade was sharp, and in short order he sawed through the bindings.

With his hands free, he tore the gag from his mouth and spit out the prodigious amount of blood that he'd been desperately trying not to swallow. After cutting the rest of his bindings, he wiped his face quickly with a sheet, then broke for the hall outside.

Though still wobbly from the pain in his jaw, a surge of adrenaline at his escape propelled him down the corridor. As he approached the heavy metal doors at the end, a portly maid carrying a bag of dirty laundry came through them from the other side. She stopped in her tracks and stared at him in shock. Weiss hobbled past her without a word. Once through the doorway, he peered back over his shoulder. She wasn't following. To keep from attracting further attention, Weiss quickly found a lavatory.

Upon seeing himself in a mirror, Weiss understood the woman's alarm. A terrifying amount of dried blood caked his beard and neck. His shirt and hands were also fouled. His left cheek was horribly swollen and bruised. He felt repulsed himself, and he gingerly washed his hands and neck as thoroughly as he could.

Weiss recoiled sharply the second he touched his left cheek with a cloth. The ache made him clench his teeth, which shot bolts of slashing pain through his skull. He cleaned up as best he could before leaving the bathroom.

Titanic's enormity now confronted Weiss directly. He was dizzy, on the verge of passing out, and could hardly visualize where he was, much less where he should go. The German staggered forward a few steps and then collapsed to the floor with his back against the wall.

How would he ever find the unfortunate person the man had infected? Moreover, how in the world would he ever find the German agent and recover the Toxic? It felt impossible. Weiss's present condition left him only one choice. He had to seek medical assistance for himself first. He couldn't do anything until he stopped the pain.

Dr. O'Loughlin opened the third-class examining room door and Weiss stumbled in, holding the side of his face.

"You have to help me . . ."

O'Loughlin squinted at Weiss's swollen jaw. "I should say," the doctor said. "Have a seat, and let's see how you are."

Weiss leaned his cane in the corner and collapsed into a chair. Dr. O'Loughlin tried to stick a thermometer in Weiss's mouth, causing the German to retch and vomit black, dead blood all over the floor. O'Loughlin recoiled.

"I've swallowed a lot of blood," Weiss said between coughs. "I'm also in terrible pain." It was a detail he would have mentioned if the surgeon hadn't been so intent with his thermometer.

"What in the devil . . . ?"

"I've been attacked and lost a tooth. I need something for the pain," Weiss said, blinking away the agony. "But that's not the sole reason I'm here."

"Attacked? On *Titanic*?" said O'Loughlin, fetching a beaker, some powders, and a glass mixing rod. He filled the container with water, mixed the solution, and poured it into a cup. "Drink this," he said. Weiss complied, feeling a measure of relief almost immediately. O'Loughlin crossed his arms. "I'll need to alert the Master-at-Arms."

"And the captain as well," Weiss replied.

O'Loughlin grunted dubiously and examined Weiss's mouth. "Good lord. It looks as if the tooth has been pulled by a butcher, not a dentist." He placed a wad of sterile gauze on the wound. "Bite down, and give that some time. The cotton should stop the bleeding and keep the socket from becoming infected. Now what about this attack?"

Where to begin? In the cold light of the doctor's office, Weiss saw how unlikely his tale would seem. Still, he had no choice. From now on, he must put his faith in the truth. He removed the gauze to speak.

"My name is Theodor Weiss. I am a doctor like you, a bacteriologist, and I was in possession of a deadly bacterium, a new strain of plague, which the German government wants to use as a weapon."

O'Loughlin blinked, and then laughed, long and loud—as if this were a joke, or Weiss were simply mad. "Of course, and I'm the man in the moon!"

"No, you must listen! The vial containing plague bacteria was stolen from me, violently, as you see. We must act quickly. I'm afraid the thief plans to expose one of the passengers. This is a mutation of the plague that decimated Manchuria. Surely you heard about it?"

The smile faded from O'Loughlin's face. "Of course. Some fifty thousand people died. But that plague was contained. It's over."

"This is not the same plague. It's a mutated version, and much worse. I was there. I . . . it's too much to explain how I have it, but you must believe me. One drop from that vial, in the mouth, the eyes, or an open wound . . . on an enclosed ship like *Titanic* . . ." Weiss's voice trailed off.

"Then help us identify your attacker," O'Loughlin said.

"I never saw his face. And he took my bag with the vial and my credentials." Weiss looked at the doctor in despair. "I have no proof, but still you must believe me. We don't have much time."

For a long moment, O'Loughlin considered the situation. "All right, tell me more about this sickness."

Weiss shifted forward in his seat eagerly. "It starts like the flu. Chills, abdominal pain, and headaches last seven to eight hours, but that's just the beginning. Then, there is a second stage. Sores appear, and a murky, infectious discharge emerges from the nose and mouth, also the ears. This progresses much more quickly, three or four hours at most." Weiss took a breath before finishing. "And in the final stage? The victim bleeds from his eyes and is lost to violent madness. Please tell me, have you seen anyone with these symptoms?"

"You mean discharge from the eyes? Certainly not!"

"Anything," Weiss said. "Dizziness, nausea?"

"I see that every day, of course. It's seasickness, not the plague. Not half an hour ago I sent a seasick cook who felt puny to rest in his quarters, simply as a precaution."

"Is this cook a veteran of the sea?"

"Yes."

"Then how is he seasick? I need to examine him."

"I assure you, Timothy is merely suffering a bout of seasickness. That or perhaps he visited a certain Southampton district prior to sailing and got more than he paid for. Time will tell."

Weiss calculated in his head. "Please, we have to treat this with the utmost urgency. If this man has been infected, he will become highly contagious within hours. Allow me to examine him."

O'Louglin bristled. "You? Examine my patient? Ridiculous."

Weiss stood and looked O'Loughlin square in the eye. "You have not seen what I have. This horror does not kill its victims. It destroys them from the inside until they lose their minds and they become insatiably violent creatures. But there's still a chance if we move now. I cannot put it any plainer than that."

O'Loughlin paused for only a moment. "We'll go to him. But don't mistake me. From this moment, *you* are the one under guard. Unless I find your plague on board, you will not see the light of day until we reach America."

14

O'Loughlin led Weiss down the third-class stairwells and past streams of passengers: gentlemen in tailored suits on their way to the smoking lounge; ladies in handsome afternoon gowns en route to the promenade deck; young people wearing modest bathing costumes searching for the swimming pool. Weiss watched them hurry along—so many that they were nearly shoulder to shoulder. Horror would rage across the populous *Titanic* if the cook was indeed infected and not found in time. Weiss would happily trade his freedom to be wrong.

Weiss and O'Loughlin arrived on Deck E and set off for Timothy's room, a shared accommodation next to places for washing potatoes and other kitchen preparations. As they passed the second-class purser's office, O'Loughlin stopped and stuck his head inside the door. "Mr. McElroy," he called. "Ring up to the bridge and have the Master-at-Arms meet us in the cooks' quarters right away."

A uniformed man with a neatly trimmed black mustache looked up from behind his mahogany counter. "May I inquire as to the purpose of your request, sir?"

"No, you may not," O'Loughlin replied.

As O'Loughlin and Weiss continued down the corridor, Weiss asked, "There are telephones aboard?"

"It's a big ship," returned O'Loughlin. "Otherwise, it would take the captain's orders half an hour to reach the boiler rooms."

The corridors were less crowded as they moved into Deck E's service areas, and Weiss picked up the pace to a half-trot. O'Loughlin stopped so he could catch his breath. He pointed to a cabin at the end of the corridor. "He'll be up there."

Weiss sprinted away, despite O'Loughlin's shout to stop. The doctor ran after the German, who stood in the doorway of an unoccupied room.

"No one's here," Weiss said.

"Why," asked O'Loughlin, "would Timothy defy my direct orders to stay in his quarters?"

Weiss studied the scene carefully. The room wasn't unlike his own, with spare bunks lining the walls on either side. Personal lockers took up much of the rest of the space. A beat-up banjo rested in the far corner. As he crossed to one of the bunks, a chattering rat scurried past and disappeared out the door.

The bottom bunk's sheets were turned down, and its pillow had a single dark stain. He examined it closely, as his heart pumped so hard it felt close to bursting from his chest. The stain was fresh and all too familiar; it could be nothing else. They'd found the person who'd been infected with the Toxic, but the cook had already progressed to stage two.

Weiss carefully examined the rest of the bed and the sheets. He found more ooze near the bottom of the pillow, indicating that the fluid had seeped from the gums. Weiss showed O'Loughlin.

"This is the discharge I told you about," said Weiss. "Do you believe me now?"

"I don't know what to believe. But something isn't right."

"This bedding will need to be burned," said the German. "Please make sure it's taken care of."

"I am not your assistant, and I will not take orders from you," huffed O'Loughlin. "We will wait for the Master-at-Arms, and he will find Timothy and determine why . . ."

Weiss wasn't listening. He'd risen to inspect the rest of the room. "More fluid," he exclaimed. "Here, on the door jamb. Don't touch it. If the fluid comes into contact with an open sore or any mucous membrane, you could be the next one infected. Scrub this down with bleach. You have rubber gloves?"

"Back in my office," O'Loughlin muttered.

"Please get them. All you have. I must find your cook."

Weiss took off down the corridor. "Come back here!" O'Loughlin called. "I order you to wait!"

By the time O'Loughlin reached the doorway, Weiss was turning the corner. O'Loughlin held back the urge to chase him. Instead, he would wait for the Master-at-Arms to handle Weiss.

———————

Tracing the cook's path proved difficult. Weiss found occasional random streaks along corridor walls, indicating that Timothy's condition was worsening. Unfortunately, the corridor split in three possible directions at regular intervals. Weiss ran this way and that, trying to pick up the trail. He was nearly ready to give up and find O'Loughlin again before noting an inky smudge leading down a stairwell.

Weiss proceeded to Deck G and an area of the ship restricted to crew. He listened carefully. There was no sound, save the hum of ice-making machines, which had left a small puddle on the floor.

An erratic pattern of wet footprints led out of the puddle to a heavy door marked "Thawing Room." Weiss pulled out his pocketwatch—it was past 5:30 P.M. By his calculations, Timothy may have been infected for up to nine hours. It was impossible to say what state his mind was in by now, but Weiss prayed the man could still reason. Fully realizing the danger, he tightened his grip on his walking stick and pulled on the door's cool metal handle with his free hand.

Weiss left the door open a crack behind him as he entered the damp, cold room. Sides of beef and racks of mutton hung from big gaff hooks in long rows. Blood dripped freely onto the floor. Some of the stains were old and dark, but not dark enough to be mistaken for the Toxic. That had a stale, dead look all its own.

Weiss squatted and scanned under the rows. The moment he confirmed Timothy's presence, his plan was to get outside quickly and bar the door. The large hunks of meat hung low to the ground and cast weighty shadows, making it tough to see. The German moved farther in, searching quietly.

The space was tight, even down the room's central passage. Weiss warily made his way down the first row. He found nothing but sides of beef hanging from their hooks. He turned to proceed down a second row, accidentally bumping into a hunk of meat. The carcass swung back and forth.

Weiss was four or five rows down, peering into a row to his right, when another carcass bumped his shoulder. He turned as a wretched pair of hands burst through and grabbed his jacket. Weiss jerked away, freeing his coat but losing his balance on the slick, bloody floor. He fell, and his walking stick went skidding away beneath the rows of meat and out of sight. Weiss looked up from the floor to find his worst fears confirmed.

The muscles in the cook's face were slack, but his eyes were wild. Rivulets of black mucus dripped from his nose and ears and dribbled over his lips. Timothy held his head in his hands, swaying with the waves of madness in his brain, banging into the meat on either side. His kitchen whites were smeared with more black stains, and in places they were torn where he must have been furiously scratching at sores.

A horrible, low sound emerged from his throat, and his mouth opened in anguish. Timothy was almost gone. There was no saving him, but the threat could end here if Weiss summoned the will to do what must be done.

Weiss's sense of responsibility trumped his fear and propelled him to his feet. He searched wildly in all directions for his weapon, but it was nowhere to be found. He looked up and saw an empty meat hook on a metal track.

The German struggled to disengage the hook, but it was thick with dried blood and reluctant to give. Timothy shuffled forward. Whether his intent was to seek help or Weiss's flesh didn't matter. Weiss pulled himself up on the hook and kicked hard into Timothy's midsection. The infected man flew backward into the sides of beef before tumbling onto the sloppy floor. He thrashed to his feet, ready to fight back like a crazed animal.

Thankfully, the swinging carcasses slowed the man's progress, and at the same time, voices could be heard outside the door. Timothy stopped, dead flat eyes turning toward the sound. Weiss gave the hook a final tug, the mechanism let go, and the gaff hook came free.

Weiss did not hesitate. He struck hard with the hook, burying it deep into the side of the cook's skull, which split as the body toppled to the floor.

Crew members burst into the room, but Weiss was oblivious to everything but destroying the infected man. Weiss withdrew the hook and slammed it into the head repeatedly, unleashing all the frustrations and fears of the previous week, of the previous year. He was no longer trying to kill a man but the specter of death itself. As Weiss raised his arm for another blow, a hand grabbed his forearm, stopping him, and then the hook was roughly yanked away.

"Murderer!" yelled a large, bearded man dressed in blood-stained butcher's whites.

Even though Weiss had killed out of necessity, the accusation was an arrow through his conscience.

The bearded man punched Weiss hard in the face, sending him reeling into the sides of beef. The butcher called to a companion to go for help and resumed taking Weiss apart, blow by blow, until he collapsed to the floor.

Moments later, O'Loughlin arrived with the Master-at-Arms and more ship's personnel.

"Good lord!" O'Loughlin exclaimed when he saw the scene. "What have you done!?"

At O'Loughlin's shoulder, the bearded man insisted, "He killed that man. I saw him do it, and a more horrible death I ne'er seen."

O'Loughlin nodded in acknowledgment but didn't reply. Instead, he donned surgical gloves and crouched down to get a better look at Timothy. Yet the German had so thoroughly destroyed the cook's skull that it was impossible to discern much of anything. Not all the fluids looked like blood, necessarily, but the light and the mess made it hard to say for sure. The stains on the cook's clothing, however, matched what O'Loughlin had seen on the bed.

"Put this man under lock and key," he said to the others crowded into the room. "Place a guard on him until you receive further orders from Captain Smith. I'll deal with the body."

Weiss raised his head, which throbbed in excruciating pain. "Doctor, tell them. Tell them about the disease. Don't touch that body, please, whatever you do."

The bearded man grunted and dragged Weiss roughly from the room.

15

"Doctor, that's an incredible story," said Captain Smith, removing his cap and leaning back into his chair. He sat at his small mahogany table with Dr. O'Loughlin and J. Bruce Ismay, whose cigar filled the room with smoke. "In your professional opinion, how much of it is true?"

Before O'Loughlin could answer, Ismay threw his smoldering cigar into an ashtray. "Why would we believe a word of it?" he sputtered. "That man is a murderer! He's trying to save his own skin!"

Ismay's shouts were loosening O'Loughlin's thin hold on his own composure. "Certain elements of the story I can confirm, Captain. Our cook did complain of the symptoms Mr. Weiss described. Of course, those symptoms are quite common. More troubling are the stains on the man's bed things and clothes. This is not blood, but some black discharge. Prudence dictates we should not dismiss the potential danger. Plagues are not to be trifled with. As for Mr. Weiss's more fantastical warnings?" The doctor tried not to think about Timothy's skull smashed against the bloody floor. "I couldn't possibly say."

"You have the devil's heart to speak such things!" came a yell from outside the captain's quarters, followed by the sound of a hard slap and a shout of pain.

The door to the captain's cabin burst open and Weiss was shoved inside. His hands, still bloody from the meat locker floor, were cuffed in front of him. A large, red handprint branded his cheek. Mr. King, the Master-at-Arms, gave Weiss a final push and roughly closed the door behind them.

Smith stood, returning his cap to his head. "You will hold your hand, Mr. King," he commanded. "I will not tolerate such behavior from my crew, no matter what this man has done."

"My apologies, Captain. I lost my temper," said King, staring at his shoes.

"So this is our murderer," said Ismay, examining Weiss's swollen face, unimposing build, and nondescript clothing. "Doesn't quite look the type, does he?"

"He goes by 'Nosworthy' on the manifest, but he's since changed his tune," replied King. "Now he's saying it's 'Weiss.' We can't be sure because he doesn't have a passport. Claims that was stolen, along with his traveling bag. This stick is also his. We found it in the meat locker where he bashed in poor Timothy's head."

King handed over Weiss's cane and Captain Smith gave it a once-over. "This is more than a stick," he said, activating the mechanism that snapped the hidden blade into view.

The captain handed the weapon back to King, who looked surprised, then angry at having his ignorance exposed. Weiss noted a formidable sword hanging on the captain's wall. The blade's battered sheath indicated the weapon wasn't merely decorative.

"What is your true name, sir?" Smith sternly addressed Weiss. "It would not be wise to make me ask a second time."

"My name is Theodor Weiss, Captain. Everything I told Dr. O'Loughlin is true. It is imperative that you . . ."

"Let's waste no more time listening to the admonitions of murderers," snapped Ismay. "We have eyewitnesses, for God's sake!"

"Sir, there is a deadly infection aboard that must be stopped," said Weiss. "Your ship and her passengers are in grave peril. Dr. O'Loughlin, as you say, is an eyewitness."

"I . . . I cannot verify your full account, sir," said O'Loughlin.

"*Titanic*'s passengers are quite safe," Ismay said to Weiss. "No one need fear a thing now that you are in custody."

Weiss mustered his dignity, held his cuffed hands in front of him, and addressed Smith. "That cook was incurably sick with a plague that could infect every passenger on this ship. I did what was necessary to stop him. We can't be sure he was the only one afflicted."

"Perhaps we should sound the general alarm!" Ismay threw up his hands theatrically. "Abandon ship!" The Master-at-Arms snickered, but was silenced by the captain's glare.

"Let me be perfectly clear," replied Weiss, looking each man in the eye, one by one. "Unless we get this quarantined immediately, there might not be anyone left to put in a lifeboat."

"Dr. O'Loughlin tells us," said Smith, "that you claim to have stolen the ingredients for this plague from the German government." He paused. "Are we all now accomplices to your crime?"

As with O'Loughlin earlier, Weiss knew his story stretched credulity, but he had to convince them. "I was working toward a cure when I discovered our military's plan to use the disease as a weapon. I had no choice but to take it, for the good of humanity. I fled Germany for America with the vial of what I refer to as "the Toxic" because I believe it might hold the key to a cure for all strains of the plague. But the Kaiser believes the Toxic belongs to him and sent an agent to intercept me. I'm sorry to say the man did his job."

"Now you claim you are the victim, and someone else is a murderer!" Ismay cried.

"I don't care whether or not you believe my story, so long as you believe that this plague has been unleashed on this ship. This man who stole the vial is unstable. I don't know how many people he may have condemned."

"If all you say is true, Mr. Weiss," the captain said, "then by not seeking the protection of my office in Southampton, you brought both a plague and a killer aboard my ship."

Embarrassment flushed Weiss's face. "Secrecy seemed the best plan." He swallowed hard. "Clearly, I was wrong."

"I don't believe a word of this. I will have you hanged," snarled Ismay. "Mr. King, lock him up for the duration."

King grabbed Weiss roughly by the arm. "Don't be a fool!" he shouted. "This plague is more than a sickness! Your passengers will become mindless fiends. They will stop at nothing except to feast on the flesh of the uninfected! They will lose their souls, their humanity—they will become like dead that walk the earth!"

The room went completely silent. Even Mr. Ismay was at a loss for words. Captain Smith stroked his ivory beard and looked hard into Weiss's eyes, searching for truth or madness.

Captain Smith spoke quietly into the silence. "What you're saying is this infection turns people into zombies."

Weiss let out a long breath, relieved not to be completely dismissed out of hand. "I have not heard that term before."

"Surely you're not taking his story seriously?" Ismay asked the captain.

"During my travels in the Caribbean, villagers sometimes told tales of the dead come to life. Naturally, I was skeptical. Yet even the wildest stories sometimes hold a kernel of truth." He turned to Weiss. "Now here you are with a similar story, told with seeming conviction. But you have only your word as evidence—you who travel under an assumed identity, carry a hidden weapon, and have brutalized a young man's head beyond recognition." Captain Smith shook his head. "I agree with Mr. Ismay. Mr. King, lock this man up."

"Finally, some sense," said Ismay. "For God's sake, get him out of sight. And above all, keep this quiet. Don't breathe a word of this beyond this room. The last thing we need is for the passengers to think that there's a madman onboard."

Weiss despaired. "Please, Captain, don't ignore this. If you do, your ship is doomed."

"I've heard your claims," Smith said curtly. "Dr. O'Loughlin, alert me instantly if you encounter any more passengers with signs of illness. Mr. King, escort Mr. . . . the German back to the cargo hold and stand guard until you receive further orders."

The Master-at-Arms rolled his head to crack his neck. "I'll make sure he don't go nowhere, Captain."

STAGE TWO

16

Titanic steamed across the Atlantic, the ship's hull cleaving a path through calm, azure waters. Smoke spilled from its stacks, leaving a misty trail above its wake. On the ship's top deck, open to the sun and clear blue sky, children shouted and laughed, having the times of their lives.

Nannies waltzed some of the wealthier boys and girls through their afternoon strolls, positioning parasols so they wouldn't be exposed to the bright sun. On the ship's starboard side, a small crowd of children gathered outside the gymnasium. Even though they had already taken their appointed turn inside, they eagerly crowded near the door for another glimpse of the exotic rowing machines, bicycles, and mechanical horses.

Below, on Deck C, still more children turned up in the barber shop with shiny coins in their fists, anxious to purchase a souvenir of their trip. Teddy bears, dolls, penknives, and official ribbons embroidered with the name *RMS Titanic* were popular ways to spend pocket money.

Passengers on the decks below were less well-dressed but the children had no less fun. Some boys swung from the baggage cranes, while others chased rats down hallways and out of stairwells. The howling lads seemed as if they would give chase till the rodents ran right off the edge of the ship.

Lou would have preferred to chase rats with the boys. But her mother wouldn't stand for such activities, and Lou was fairly certain the boys wouldn't be keen on having a girl join them. Boys were like that. So instead, she made do with a dull group of girls about her age in the third-class common room, pretending to make tea for rag dolls and providing make-believe medicine for their tummy aches. Lou's mother, satisfied that the girl had learned her lesson about talking to strange gentlemen, went to the library to write letters to family.

Lou listlessly dressed and undressed a rag doll, looking for something, *anything* else to occupy her time. Thinking her mother would be safely occupied in the library for at least an hour, Lou took a stroll to see what she could find. She noticed a sign that read "Squash Court Observation Deck" and decided to have a look.

These people dress better to watch a game than I do to go to Sunday church, Lou marveled, surveying the gathered crowd. Even the players on the court were dressed smartly in spotless white shorts and shirts. A quick, guarded smell of her dress confirmed that she didn't stink; she hadn't changed clothes since their first day on board. Her mother was saving her other good outfit for when they arrived in New York.

Lou was thrilled to spot Lady Cardeza, hair and all, chattering not far away. Few in the room were paying the woman much attention. They seemed more interested in squash than gossip. With a sniff, Lady Cardeza announced loudly, "I have multiple concerns to attend, unlike those who have nothing to do but play silly games!" Then she left. Lou imagined "multiple concerns" meant changing into a new dress from one of her fourteen trunks.

"Say," one man next to Lou said, "who's up next?"

His companion, a man with an enormous walrus mustache, replied, "Thomas Andrews and Fred Wright."

"Who's Andrews? A professional as well?"

"Hardly. He designed *Titanic*. That's him over there."

Andrews stood off in a far corner, frowning at a piece of trim above the observation window. He started writing in a small pad of paper.

"*He's* going to take on Fred Wright? That little fellow doesn't stand a chance!"

"I hear Andrews is an accomplished player, but agreed. Wright will wear him down."

Lou watched as Andrews put away his notebook and made his way to the court to warm up for the match. He darted this way and that, provoking laughter from the two gentlemen. Lou thought he looked agile and quick. Wright, practicing his powerful shots, seemed like a statue by comparison.

"Hey mister," Lou said. "My money would be on Andrews."

The two men turned, surprised to hear a young girl putting forth a challenge. The first chuckled under his breath. "A proper lady doesn't gamble," he chided. "Besides, you don't look like you've got anything to bet with."

Lou felt her ears get hot, just like when the boy tried to take her corner for selling papers. She drew herself up. "Oh I've got money, sir, my word on that. How much you want to make it? Say a shilling?"

The man with the walrus mustache laughed loudly. The first man gripped the lapels of his jacket. "If you want a wager, young lady, I deal by the pound."

"A pound it is then," Lou said, sticking out her bottom lip.

The man with the mustache was beside himself with laughter. "What kind of sport are you, taking a pound from a child?" He pointed down to the court where Andrews was shaking hands with his much taller and brawnier opponent. "Look at the difference between them."

Lou gulped at the disparity. She was on the line for six months' wages.

17

Almost an entire day had passed since Weiss had been locked in the cargo hold, and he didn't know whether to be relieved or alarmed that no one had yet let him out. Surely, if there had been new cases of the disease, someone would have come for him. Weiss understood only too well that enough time had passed for the infection to spread and for the disease to work its horrific transformation.

And what of his attacker? He was still in possession of the vial, its contents deadly but possibly holding the key to a cure. Weiss had to get out, and he had spent more hours than he cared to count devising fruitless escape plans. His hands were still cuffed in front of him. The hatch door in the ceiling above was locked tight. No one had visited him but Mr. King, who had brought Weiss one meal that morning and had promised to bring another. The weapon options at his disposal seemed almost comical: the room was piled with wooden crates, variously bearing the names of concerns such as *Acker, Merrall & Condit* and *Lasker & Bernstein,* which contained only useless items such as anchovies, sponges, and ostrich feathers.

Not to mention, Mr. King was larger by half a foot and fifty pounds at least, and as he liked to point out, he made a living out of "beating down bums." The scientist was unlikely to overpower him or play on his sympathies. Mr. King had none regarding his captive.

Mr. King had led Weiss down a series of stairwells bustling with crew members after his audience with the captain and Mr. Ismay. Weiss walked slowly and deliberately, searching the passing faces for signs of infection.

"Keep walking or by God I'll disobey the captain's orders. You'll arrive at the bottom of these stairs in a righteous hurry," promised King. "Don't think I won't enjoy watching you bounce a couple times after I grab your no-good neck and send you sailing."

A shilling-sized spot of black fluid on the next landing stopped Weiss short. "That's what I've been trying to warn you about," Weiss said. "There! The Toxic!"

The Master-at-Arms pushed Weiss out of the way and got down on one knee. King studied the glistening black bead for a moment before looking up. A broad, satisfied smile creased his face as he ran his index finger through the globule.

"Dear God," Weiss admonished, "don't touch that. You'll become— what did Captain Smith say? *A zombie!*"

King laughed and stood up. With his unstained hand, he grabbed the chain of Weiss's handcuffs and pulled him close. "Are you referrin' to this?" King barked, shoving his blackened digit two inches from Weiss's nose. The German arched back in fear, slamming into the wall. Mr. King pinned him against it.

"It's oil, you fool!" King pointed toward the ceiling. "There are huge cranes and fans on the deck above us. They use oil. Oil!"

Weiss took a hard look at the drop. King was right.

"So much for your story," he scoffed. Then he wiped his finger on Weiss's cheek and delivered on his promise to make the German's trip down the steps a short one.

Where is King, anyway? Weiss now thought. He was hungry for news. He'd gladly suffer more of his jailer's abuse for confirmation that all was well. *Do I dare believe the worst is over?*

Suddenly, heavy, awkward footsteps sounded outside and above. With a heavy metallic *thunk*, the hatch door shook, then swung open, and someone started descending the ladder. It was Mr. King. His motions were clumsy, and when he reached the bottom, he turned and tripped, spilling a tray he held in one hand. Food, a plate, cutlery, and a mug of coffee tumbled and spilled across the floor, but King remained slumped on the ground, saying nothing.

Weiss eyed him warily. "Mr. King?" he asked.

King lifted his head, mumbled, and coughed hard. Black spittle clung to his lips. A cold shiver ran up Weiss's neck. "Mr. King, you're sick! Let me help you."

King's face contorted, and he pressed his palms against his temples.

Weiss crept nearer. Black fluid dripped from King's nose. A wicked sore was visible at the base of his neck, just inside his collar.

King grimaced and groaned more violently, then he coughed again. Weiss jumped back as dark mucus sprayed out.

"*Make it stop!*" King shouted, grabbing the dropped coffee mug and throwing it to shatter against the wall.

Nothing can stop it now, Weiss thought, but he said, "How long has it been since you saw the black fluid, Mr. King? How long? Where have you been? Who have you been in contact with?" With each question, Weiss backed farther away till he bumped into a stack of crates. "Did someone do this to you? I have to know where you've been!"

The Master-at-Arms vomited a viscous stream of dark liquid over his uniform. His skin was pale. When he raised his head, his eyes turned glassy and dark tears streamed out the sides.

"Mr. King!" Weiss yelled in desperation, holding up his bound hands. "Remember, you are a man!"

King bowed his head again, and for a long terrible moment, there was silence in the cargo hold. Then an excruciating moan rose in his throat, undulating louder and stronger, until the thing that had once been Mr. King rose on unsteady legs. Weiss and the creature regarded each other, and then Weiss made a leap for the hatch ladder. The zombie lunged to meet him, and the scientist narrowly sidestepped his grasp. The confined, crowded space left little room for maneuvering. Weiss raced behind a stack of crates, listening for King's following footsteps.

When Weiss heard the shuffling gait nearing, he put his shoulder into the pile of wooden boxes. With a heavy crash, the crates fell atop Mr. King, whose head landed violently on the metal floor. The Master-of-Arms lay still and Weiss exhaled.

Then a plank of wood groaned and cracked loudly, and Weiss watched incredulously as King moaned, low and pained, and raised himself up onto his elbows. A deep gash cleaved the skin above his right eye, but he didn't seem to notice. Seeing Weiss, King moaned louder still, mouth agape, and got to his feet once more. Weiss darted past and leaped for the ladder. He pulled his feet up onto the first rung, but his bound hands stymied further progress. In desperation, he released both hands at once and tried to grab a higher rung, only to miss and tumble backward to the floor.

Weiss looked up in horror to find the zombie standing over him. The creature lunged. From his back, Weiss frantically jammed the chain of his handcuffs into the hideous mouth, holding off the putrid, black-stained teeth with all his might.

He heard the sound of the hatch above creak open. "Mr. King!" someone shouted, and then Captain Smith, with sword swinging at his side, slid down the ladder in one fluid motion, not touching a single rung along the way. The zombie relented and peered hard at the captain, who grimaced at the sight of his former charge. Smith drew the blade in a flash and cleaved deeply into the zombie's neck. A second blow fully decapitated Smith's former Master-at-Arms, whose head bounced twice on the floor.

10

Lou was quite late getting back to her cabin. She had been gone the entire day and missed two meals. That was not unusual when she was selling papers, but that was her old life, the one her mother insisted on leaving behind. This kind of absence wouldn't be tolerated aboard *Titanic*. Lou pouted. *She's the one who wanted me out playing with those dainty nincompoops in the first place. How can I help it if I found something better to do and couldn't tear myself away?*

Perhaps the two pounds buttoned inside her dress pocket would smooth things over. Lou fingered the notes, still not quite believing what had happened. It was thanks to Mr. Andrews, whose focused, agile shots kept his bigger adversary scrambling until he doubled over, gasping for breath. Andrews wore down the professional, not the other way around, as Lou's condescending opponent had wagered. She even baited the wealthy fool to go in a second time, doubling her winnings.

When Andrews's matches were over and Lou's prize had been collected—she could still hear the man with the walrus mustache guffawing inside her head—she continued to eavesdrop on the conversations of upper-class passengers that swirled around the observation deck. She knew she should return to her cabin, but she couldn't tear herself away from talk of political scandal and high finance. It was her news-papers come to life!

New matches and intriguing exchanges continued right until the court closed. Only when the lights shut off did Lou high-tail it for home. It had been an exhilarating and even lucrative day.

As Lou scuffled out of a stairwell and hustled toward her cabin, she rehearsed how to present her earnings and the events of the day in such a way that her mother wouldn't be angry. It would take a deft hand, but Lou was experienced finding ways out of trouble. Her mother wanted Lou to leave her tomboy ways behind in Brighton, so she would burst in and describe what a cultured and refined day she'd had: how she'd acted like a lady and then got the better of the estab-lished businessmen.

A murmur down the corridor stopped her just short of her own cabin door. Fifteen cabins away was a man, his head hung so low that Lou couldn't make out his face. The fellow appeared drunk, bumbling stiffly down the corridor. Lou knew how to handle drunks. They com-plained about the news in the paper and often weren't keen on paying for it. The best strategy was to ignore them, even walk away if you needed to. She scampered inside her cabin door before the moaning sot saw her.

The cabin was dark, but Lou did not turn on the light. How long had her mother been asleep? Lou quietly locked the door, hoping to crawl into bed without notice and claim a much earlier arrival. As she tiptoed to her bunk, her mother stirred.

"Mama?" Lou whispered. Her mother didn't reply, but her breath-ing was thick, almost like snoring. She snored on occasion (though she always denied it); it meant she was exhausted and sleeping deeply. Lou felt in the dark for the small ladder leading to the top bed. She found a rung and began climbing silently. Then, halfway up, a cold hand wrapped around her ankle. She tried to pull away, but the grip was tight.

"I did what you said, Mama, and played rag dolls at first, and then I went to the squash courts. I was very proper and polite, and I conversed with two investment bankers and watched the ladies . . ." The fist continued pulling on her, unyielding. "And I won two pounds, Mama! On the game. I won two whole pounds!"

The hand jerked hard, causing Lou to fall off the ladder. She landed on the floor with a thud, pained and surprised. She gathered herself and scooted over to the light switch. She turned it on.

Lou's mother was climbing out of bed, her head hung low like the drunk in the hall. Black ink had spilled all over the front of her white nightgown. Her hands, always white as porcelain, were bruised and gnarled into menacing hooks. She was . . . *wrong*.

"I'm sorry, Mama!" Lou pleaded. "I didn't mean to be gone all day!"

Lou's mother raised her head, revealing a face riddled with black sores. One of the lenses in her spectacles was shattered into a spider's web, and the eye beneath contained no remnant of her mother. She was twisted and horrible, and crying black tears.

Dark spittle oozed from her mother's mouth. Then she moaned in agony and lashed out at her daughter.

Lou screamed.

19

Dr. William O'Loughlin paced the length of the sitting room, pulling hard on a cigarette as Captain Smith's emergency team assembled. Chief Officer Henry Wilde and First Officer William Murdoch joined Thomas Andrews and Theodor Weiss. J. Bruce Ismay, the last to arrive, stopped short and bristled at the presence of the German.

"I fail to understand," Ismay said, "why this murderer is still among us."

"Mr. Weiss brought this infection aboard," Captain Smith said brusquely, "and he'll damn well help us get rid of it. We need his expertise. I will not allow my ship to be overwhelmed."

"And I say lock him up for his crimes," Ismay retorted. "Remember who hired you, Captain."

"And you may relieve me of my duties when we dock safely." Smith turned his attention to the rest of the men. "As some of you know, a horrible plague has infected *Titanic,* and we must take action immediately. I was skeptical of Mr. Weiss's claims at first, but I regret to say that I have now seen the zombies myself. God help me, I have already been forced to kill four times, including our poor Mr. King."

"Zombies?" replied Officer Wilde.

Ismay said weakly, "You killed King?"

"King was a man no more," said Smith.

"I saw King just this morning . . . " protested Officer Murdoch.

"King is dead," said the captain, "and at my hand."

"A man can't be killed just because he's turned ill!" said Murdoch.

"You're not listening," said Smith. "King wasn't 'ill.' He had turned into a monster."

"With all due respect, Captain, saying there's a disease aboard is one thing," Officer Wilde said, trying to sound reasonable. "But this 'monster' talk is hard to swallow."

Dr. O'Loughlin piped up. "Seeing is believing."

O'Loughlin lifted a heavy canvas sea bag from beneath the table and set it on top with a heavy thump. He donned a pair of sterilized medical gloves, carefully loosened the cinched cord at the top of the bag, and rolled its contents onto the table.

Mr. Andrews made a retching sound and excused himself to the captain's lavatory. Ismay also choked. The rest of the men simply looked on in horror.

The severed, grotesquely transformed head of Mr. King was terrifying. His eyes were open and staring into the void, sunk into hollows the color of violaceous bruises. Dark, dried fluid and blood stained his features and matted his hair. Though King had been dead only a few hours, his forehead was already rotting, and the gash above his eye had widened to expose ivory skull bone. Worst of all was the smell—a noxious odor of decaying meat and death, but somehow fouler yet, as if fired with Hell's sulfur.

"My God," managed Ismay. "It's true."

"No one touch it!" Weiss snapped. "If that fluid finds a way into your bloodstream, you could become infected, even now."

All the men but O'Loughlin took a step back. No one said a word. Dr. O'Loughlin straightened his spine and, with a muffled cough, returned King's head to the canvas bag.

Captain Smith stood. "The three infected were found in the aft of Deck E," he said. "That seems to be where the disease has taken hold. Our mission is clear: We must take measures to make sure a proper quarantine is in place."

"What makes you so sure this madman won't release more on other parts of the ship?" asked Dr. O'Loughlin.

"Neither the agent nor the Germans have any reason to infect *Titanic*'s passengers," said Weiss. "He simply needed to authenticate the vial's contents. Now that he has, he needs to escape with as much of the Toxic as possible to satisfy the German military."

"Quarantine it is, then," said O'Loughlin. "What kind of time do we have here?"

"The infection cycle runs in three stages, taking anywhere from seven to fourteen hours, depending on how long it takes for the sickness to reach the brain," Weiss said. "If we act quickly, math may be on our side. We know of five cases so far, and all the infected have been killed. The contaminated areas have been thoroughly cleaned. It might be too much to hope, but Captain Smith may have stopped the outbreak altogether."

"I'm not as optimistic," said O'Loughlin, clearing his throat with difficulty. "Who knows what kind of trail of black fluid the men have left behind? I've cleaned what I've found, but that might not be all."

"Forgive me for pointing out the obvious," interrupted Ismay, "but why are we listening to Mr. Weiss, if that's truly his name, and treating him as if he's some sort of medical dignitary? By his own admission, he has brought a disease on board that could kill us all! Who's to say he isn't the very same 'German agent' he's warning us about? Can he prove he's not? Perhaps he's trying to turn *Titanic* into some kind of weapon against New York City itself!"

For a moment, each man looked to Weiss, who shifted uncomfortably. Then he squared his shoulders and said defiantly, "If you doubt my veracity, lock me up again. I have no further proof, and every moment we spend arguing my credibility only gives the disease more time to spread. We're dealing with a fast-acting contagion, closed quarters, and a heavily populated ship. For God's sake, stop talking and act now!"

Captain Smith stood. "Mr. Ismay, I agree. Mr. Weiss has much to answer for, but this is not the time. We must first contain this disease, and swiftly. Mr. Wilde, you will assign a crew of our strongest able seamen to accompany Mr. Weiss, Mr. Andrews, and myself down to Deck E. Once there, we will do our level best to isolate the healthy and lock up any infected persons until we reach New York."

"Captain, the sick must be destroyed," said Weiss. "There is no cure, and they'll only infect more!"

"*You* have no cure," said Ismay. "We'll find out what American scientists say when we get to New York."

"Mr. Andrews," said the captain, ignoring the bickering. "Deck plans, if you would."

Still pale, Andrews returned from the lavatory. The ship's designer retrieved a canister from the corner of the room and pulled out a set of schematic drawings, with separate pages for each of *Titanic*'s ten decks. Seven decks above propulsion crew areas held passenger cabins, with Deck E right in the middle. He unfurled the Deck E plan, and the men closed around it.

Andrews said, "Deck E is one of the most heavily populated areas on *Titanic*. A very dangerous place for an epidemic."

"Our hope is that the disease is contained among passengers located here," said the captain, pointing to a series of third-class cabins lining both sides of the ship's aft.

Andrews pulled a grease pencil from behind his ear. "There are five ways to access Deck E from the aft part of the ship," he noted, making a series of circles on the blueprints. "We'll need two men at each of these stairwells, as well as this elevator. That should provide safety for passengers on the three decks above, and if we do our jobs well, on the three decks below."

"Many of the men are off duty for the night," cautioned Wilde. "Some will be sleeping, some might need to sleep off their evening, if you get my meaning. It might take some time to assemble and coordinate such a sizable team."

"Then get at it," said Captain Smith. "If we're quick about our work, we should be able to assess the danger and, if necessary, enact our quarantine before the passengers start waking for the day."

"And just how do you propose to do that?" asked Ismay, unbuttoning his top collar button.

"With welding torches from the Deck E electrical supply," Smith replied. "We'll use a porter's key to access the rooms. If the passengers inside show signs of the illness . . ."

"Surely we won't imprison them inside," protested Andrews, who was reminded of the stories of "the Tomb."

"In lieu of other, more permanent measures," said Weiss, "locking them inside their cabins is in the best interests of every healthy person on the ship."

None of this sat well with Ismay. "What do you expect me to communicate to the rest of the passengers who request access to their bought-and-paid-for amenities on the lower decks?" he asked. "And what about the healthy? Surely they won't remain trapped with the sick!"

"We may have to set up some sort of area for them, perhaps in the second-class dining hall," Dr. O'Loughlin offered.

"Certainly not!" said Ismay. "Imagine the press! The gossip!"

"If this disease spreads," replied Smith, "the press will be the least of our worries." Ismay reddened but said nothing.

"Mr. Wilde, you will man the bridge," ordered the captain. "Mr. Murdoch, assemble an arsenal consisting of guns, clubs, and whatever else might serve. Just in case matters are worse than we anticipate."

"If I may, Captain?" said Mr. Andrews. "I think it's important that we give the able seamen joining us a healthy fear of what they could face down below."

With his grease pencil, Andrews drew a line through "Deck E" atop his deck plans. Then with a careful architect's hand, he wrote in a new name for the infected area: Deck Z.

20

Exposed on all sides to the elements and frigid air hovering above the Atlantic, *Titanic*'s bridge should have been uncomfortably cold for anyone without a heavy coat. But for J. Bruce Ismay, a dinner jacket provided more than adequate protection. In fact, it felt a little stifling as he paced the open area in front of the ship's wheelhouse. The ramifications of the captain's meeting were sinking in, and they fueled Ismay's fire.

Titanic's maiden voyage was to be a triumphant confirmation of his business acumen, his decisiveness, his talent, his intuitive eye for the future. Building *Titanic* was his master stroke, capturing several lucrative areas of transatlantic shipping all at once. Shuttling passengers across the Atlantic was an obvious source of revenue, but the contracts for hauling mail and beef, of all things, were profitable as well.

Ismay loved a good game of pool, and he had maneuvered his father's company into a spot at the biggest game of shipping billiards in the world, with giant players like J.P. Morgan betting that Ismay could beat all comers. Finally, he was in position to run the table! But now, he saw that the German's cursed plague could cause a horrible miscue. One scratch would destroy all he'd worked for. He wasn't about to let that happen.

Ismay believed the plague's threat was real—Mr. King's head was all the evidence he needed for that. But after giving it some thought, he found Captain Smith's plan lacking. *Titanic* was the most powerful force in the Atlantic, and by God, he would use its muscle to get them out of this fix. At a speed of 22 knots or higher, *Titanic* could reach New York on Monday, ahead of schedule and during the dead of night. An army of White Star security, if necessary, could deal with any sick passengers away from the prying eyes of newspapermen.

Chief Officer Henry Wilde was at the helm as Ismay approached. He said discreetly, "I want additional boilers lit. Increase our speed to seventy-eight revolutions at once. We're not sitting atop this much power to float across the sea like a stick of driftwood."

Wilde responded in a firm, low voice. "Those are not the orders I received from the captain, sir."

"Mr. Wilde," Ismay replied, "those are the orders on the bridge now."

"Perhaps we'd better speak privately, sir," recommended Wilde, and he gently led Ismay away from the other men. Ismay did Captain Smith's second-in-command the courtesy of following him out onto the relative privacy of the deck.

Standing under a moonless sky, Wilde said, "I understand your position in all this, Mr. Ismay, but . . ."

"Mr. Wilde, you were at that meeting," interrupted Ismay. "You saw what was left of Mr. King. So you must have arrived at the same conclusion I have: We need to get to New York as quickly as possible."

"Yes, sir, of course, but . . ."

"But nothing. What's our best chance? To muddle along in the water, hoping to outlast whatever horror is aboard? Or to steam hard for New York, where we can evacuate the ship? I know the captain didn't give you a direct order to increase speed, and I appreciate your respect of maritime tradition, but sometimes the rulebook must be revised to fit the situation."

"Sir, in times of emergency, only *the captain* has the prerogative to rewrite the rulebook."

"And in his absence, Mr. Wilde, *you* are captain. Smith is on his way down into the bowels of this ship to risk life and limb for it, and we're all in his debt. Do you really want to keep arguing against using the full powers of the greatest seafaring vessel ever created? The longer we're at sea, the more time this thing has to spread. Running at full capacity is the only way Smith or any of us is going to survive this voyage."

Without giving Wilde a chance to respond, Ismay turned and walked back toward the bridge. The ploy worked.

The chief officer followed him into the wheelhouse. "Alert the firemen," ordered Wilde, straightening his cap, "and tell them to light as many additional boilers as necessary to achieve top speed."

"Excellent," said Ismay, then he added loud enough for all to hear, "Men, we're about to set a new record for crossing the Atlantic. Do your job, do it well, and you'll be the toast of New York."

Ismay felt satisfied. Yet again, he had acted boldly and effectively. His play had been well thought out and executed. Now the balls just had to roll into place.

21

Dr. O'Loughlin coughed. Rancid phlegm filled his throat. He was packing his medical bag to join the captain's quarantine party on Deck E. He quickly removed his handkerchief from his jacket pocket and expectorated into it. He looked down to find his death sentence.

On the white cloth, the great gob of mucus was stained black. Hours earlier he'd felt the onset of what he considered exhaustion, perhaps only a cold. Now he knew better.

O'Loughlin understood the way his story would end. Indeed, was the examination of King's severed head how he'd been infected? He had worn gloves and taken every precaution. *There's much about this sickness that Mr. Weiss still does not understand*, he thought bitterly.

O'Loughlin's bones ached as he slowly made his way down the promenade deck. At least he would have some say in the way things played out. And why shouldn't he? The doctor was an orphan, raised by an uncle long since passed; there were no blood ties to be concerned with. *William Francis Norman O'Loughlin*. His parents had gone to an awful lot of trouble thinking up names before leaving him to fend for himself in the world.

He had never married, and at age sixty-two, there was little likelihood he ever would. There had been women, yes, but after forty years at sea, they were mostly of the "ships passing in the night" variety. *Married to the sea*, O'Loughlin often thought. Tonight he would tie that knot hard and fast.

To think he'd initially refused service on *Titanic,* having been quite content with his duties on *Olympic.* The doctor had discussed those reservations with his friend Mr. Andrews. "I'm too tired at this time of life," O'Loughlin argued, "to be waltzing from one ship to another."

"You're old, true enough, but no need to be lazy as well," Andrews had chided. "Pack your bags and have an adventure." O'Loughlin relented and agreed to serve aboard *Titanic.*

It had been his job to examine the crew muster sheets with the immigration officer from the Board of Trade. "It's a healthy crew," O'Loughlin had pronounced, which had been accurate at the time.

Given that his symptoms weren't yet severe, O'Loughlin determined he was still early in the infection cycle. But he couldn't confess to his malady. *Captain Smith would lock me in a cabin, where I'd turn into a ghoul.* It served no purpose telling anyone, not even Andrews. Good-byes were never a strong suit.

Weiss and the rest would have to identify the sick on Deck E on their own. O'Loughlin would defy his captain's command in order to follow an oath he'd taken long ago: to first and above all else, do no harm. There was only one way to keep that promise.

Arriving at the railing, the surgeon reached inside his coat, withdrew a bottle of well-aged rye he saved for special occasions, and pulled the cork with his front teeth. He leaned over the bar, peering down at the black water rushing beneath *Titanic.* He took a long swig and quickly spat it out—his personal brand of medicine had turned on him. It now tasted acrid and bitter to his diseased tongue.

He kissed the bottle—he didn't know why, perhaps for luck?—before flinging it into the sea. And then William Francis Norman O'Loughlin jumped.

22

"Mr. Clench. Good to see that you've finally sobered enough to join us," snapped the captain.

Joe Clench, a seaman who looked to be strong as an anchor and nearly as heavy, belched. Squinting at the light, he joined three other rugged able seamen by the names of Harry Holman, Bertram Terrell, and George McGough.

The men, along with the captain, Weiss, and Andrews, huddled in the stairwell outside Deck Z. They were outfitted with buckskin officers' gloves, and were dressed to expose as little flesh as possible. Each possessed assorted clubs and cudgels for the night's work, which were tucked into belts and pockets. Captain Smith also distributed short-barreled Webley handguns, the words "White Star Lines" ornately etched into them. Andrews had taken his carefully—it was his first time holding a firearm.

"This has all taken far too long. We have to pick up the pace," said Captain Smith.

"What about O'Loughlin?" asked Andrews.

Captain Smith pushed the men on. "There's no more time to wait, and no time to search for him," he said. "If O'Loughlin's not here, he must have good reason. We're going in."

Weiss, Andrews, and Smith, followed by the able seamen, stepped through heavy doors and into an open foyer that surrounded the stairwell.

Passenger cabins lined the outside walls of the foyer, forming a box around the stairwell. The complete lack of noise was unsettling, even eerie, despite the early hour. The able seamen lit gas lanterns, sending flickering light dancing against cabin doors. Smith broke the quiet with a voice low and urgent. "Remember, men: Should a sleeping—and healthy—passenger wake up in a huff while you're inspecting their room, explain that it's a routine safety check. Leave the healthy to sleep until we determine the extent of the danger."

"But if you find something, anything like the symptoms I've described to you," said Weiss, "call my name immediately." By the scowls on the able seamen's faces, it was clear they weren't keen on taking orders from a passenger.

"I can handle those things without your help," mumbled Clench.

"Listen up, Mr. Clench," said the captain. "These creatures aren't as easy to stop as you seem to believe, especially for a man in your condition."

Clench held up a meaty fist. "This ought to do the trick."

"You'll be a dead man if you try," warned Weiss. "No, worse. This disease is spread when that black fluid gets in your system. If you cut your hand splitting some zombie's lip, you'll be as good as gone."

Clench's face soured. "If we can't touch 'em, how do you expect to stop 'em?"

"If you're attacked," Captain Smith said, "dispatch them with your firearm."

"And aim for their heads," Weiss added. "I can tell you from hard experience: firing at the chest won't slow zombies down but for a moment. To fully dispatch these creatures, you must destroy the brains."

"Blimey," whispered seaman Holman, eyes half-hidden beneath a navy-blue knit cap.

"Bullets straight between the eyes, men," commanded Smith. "Leave nothing to chance."

"I must confess," Andrews interrupted. "I don't know if I could bring myself to shoot someone in cold blood."

Clench pushed his cap back in disgust. "Can I suggest, Cap'n," he said, "that we send Johnny Grease Pencil up top. I, for one, wouldn't want to be caught in a scrape with this fellow by my side."

Andrews drew himself up to full height, which was a good six inches below Clench's. "Are you calling me a coward, sir?"

"A coward runs from a fight," said Clench, eyes narrowing. "I don't believe you've ever seen one."

"I'm not running now," said Andrews, glaring up at Clench. Andrews adjusted his bowler hat, the one he wore to communicate authority. Its effectiveness was lessened by his baby face.

The seaman brought his shoulders back, and feinted a blow. Andrews flinched, prompting a guffaw from Clench and the other sailors.

"We've no time for this, Mr. Clench, *no time*," barked the captain.

"Don't mean nothin' by it," laughed Clench.

"Yes, let's get on with the task at hand," said Andrews, attempting to recover his dignity.

Weiss said, "Remember, if you run out of bullets, use your truncheons. Bludgeon the zombie's skull."

The able seamen grunted. Andrews turned to the captain with concern. "No pistol for you, Sir?"

"I'll defend myself without one," Smith replied. "It's time, men. Go quietly, door to door. If you find anything out of the ordinary, call for Mr. Weiss so he can evaluate the situation."

The men nodded, fanning out in different directions to search the cabins in the foyer. They inserted their passkeys, lightly turned them in the locks, and slipped into the rooms with lanterns held high.

Less than a minute later, Seaman Holman called out in an exaggerated whisper, "Mr. Weiss, I think you should have a look in here."

Weiss broke for the door, surprised at how little time it took for him to be summoned. Then he heard his name called again, in quick succession three more times.

"Mr. Weiss."

"Mr. Weiss."

"Mr. Weiss."

He continued into Seaman Holman's room. Weiss pushed open the half-closed door with a damp palm. The lantern's faint glow drew him to a bunk on the cabin's right.

"Here, sir," whispered Holman. Weiss moved closer.

The lantern rattled anxiously in Holman's shaking hand. Black splotches dotted a white sheet like a Dalmatian's coat. Weiss carefully pulled back the sheet to reveal a woman, her face fouled with black sores. She reached up for the men.

"Please," she said, burping up black bile, "my baby, you have to help her!" She gestured toward the other bunk and then grabbed both her ears, grimacing in pain.

Weiss moved quickly to the other bed and pulled back another black-stained sheet. A little girl lay curled in the fetal position, her face looking angelic and unmarred. *Perhaps she's been spared,* thought Weiss. He gently turned her over, only to find sodden sores oozing on her hidden side. He pulled back and gestured for Holman to join him in the hall. The infected woman was too overwhelmed with her own struggles to notice them leave.

Outside two of the able seaman men waited, along with the captain and Andrews.

"We've all found signs of infection," Smith said gravely.

"It . . . it shouldn't be possible," insisted Weiss. "One cook couldn't have started such an avalanche."

"Nevertheless, there is not an uninfected person among five rooms so far," said the captain. "Perhaps your agent infected more people than you suspect."

"Perhaps," conceded Weiss, "but it makes no sense. What purpose would it serve to infect more passengers? That compromises his mission and puts the man himself in danger!"

"Yet this area's infected all the same," Captain Smith replied as his thought was punctuated with a loud crash, followed by a flash and the *whhhuff* of igniting fuel.

The men raced into a corridor leading off the foyer to find the floor aflame around Seaman Terrell. He had dropped his lantern while trying desperately to shut a cabin door. A plague-infected woman was wedged between door and frame and getting the better of the sailor. "It's one of 'em," Terrell yelled. "Full-blown one of 'em!"

Andrews removed his coat and beat the flames out while McGough, Clench, and Holman threw themselves against the door. The zombie seemed immune to pain, hissing and moaning as the four strong men leaned on the door hard enough to crack her ribs.

"Let the door open," commanded Smith, calmly unsheathing his sword.

"But Cap'n . . . !" protested Clench.

"Open it!"

In unison, the men released the door, and it flew open. In the same instant, Captain Smith stepped forward and struck, removing the woman's head with his blade as she stumbled out. Her head hit the floor and rolled to a stop at Weiss's feet. It still wore spectacles with a single broken lens.

"Dear God, I know this woman," Weiss said. He bolted to the open door and looked inside in a panic. "Where's her daughter? Where's Lou?"

"No one else was in there, Mr. Weiss," said Terrell. "I thought the room empty at first. Then I heard something under the bunk so I went to take a look. She was under there all right, rootin' around like she was lookin' for something. Then she came at me."

Andrews finished slapping the last flame and cautioned, "If it can be helped, let's please not break any more lanterns. Kerosene burns hot."

"Point taken, Mr. Andrews," said the captain. "Now, how far along were the ones that you men saw in the other cabins? Were they in the same shape as this woman?"

"Not a whole lot different."

"Two were thrashin' around on their beds, they were."

"Mine were asleep, but that black stuff ran out their faces."

"Clench, take these men for the blowtorches," said the captain.

"The electrical supply room's down past two watertight doors on your right, not five minutes away," said Andrews, "right before you get to the turbine engine casing. You'll know it by the rumbling."

"I expect your return straight away," ordered the captain. "The situation is worse than we feared. We need to start sealing doors now."

Clench grunted and took off down the corridor with the other able seamen close behind.

"Keep a lookout for a girl, about eleven years old with wild hair!" shouted Weiss after them. "She's a friend of mine!"

Smith turned to Weiss. "Could it be possible that we already have a whole deck foul with zombies?"

Weiss shrugged grimly and stooped to examine the woman's body. He could see no bite marks, no gaping wounds, no signs of attack. How had the bacteria entered her system? It didn't make sense, yet there was little doubt that Deck Z had been aptly named as more doors began to open.

23

Joe Clench led the able seamen past the first watertight door down the narrow hallway to the storage room, pistol drawn and grumbling all the way. "You ask me, Captain Smith has this all wrong. If there's more o' those things to fight, we should be the ones doin' the fightin'. Who's going to fend off the next one of those zombie-monsters, the git with the slide rule?"

"Torch tanks are heavy, Clench—don't expect the little fella could handle one," sneered Holman.

McGough and Terrell sniggered, but truth be told they preferred retrieving welding torches to another battle with monsters. If Mr. Andrews or Mr. Weiss wanted a go, they could have it. All was calm as the able seamen made their way. Even so, Seaman Holman, as last in line, warily surveyed the hall behind them, his White Star gun at the ready.

Clench wiped his brow with the sleeve of his blue denim shirt. His wool flannel underthings were just right for work on the boat deck, but they were a damned nuisance below; he was too hot by half. He reached the door to the storage room and tucked his pistol into the back of his pants. "Time to haul, boys," he grunted as he pushed open the door.

There must have been a dozen of them inside the large storage room, feeding on an unfortunate porter who'd come down for a replacement light switch. The creatures were formerly engineers from the looks of their black jackets and white trousers, now discolored from the chaos raging in their bodies. Sickly moans caromed off the corridor walls as the zombies brutally assaulted the seamen. Five of the fiends were atop Joe Clench before the door was fully open. He drove two ghouls against the doorframe, audibly cracking their bones, but he had no way to stop more jaws from latching onto his shoulder, arm, and neck. Though Clench thrashed mightily, within seconds he was overwhelmed.

As more zombies emerged from the room, Terrell and McGough aimed their weapons into the zombies' decaying midsections, completely forgetting Weiss's instructions. By chance, two zombies were struck in the head and destroyed, but they were simply trampled over by others in stained white sailor's caps cocked at crazy angles. Terrell was savagely mauled, as three zombies shoved at one another for the chance to tear into his flesh and brain. McGough emptied his gun into a single assailant, a former junior assistant engineer still wearing wire-rim spectacles and not more than twenty years old. The last shot took the thing's ear off, but the junior engineer overpowered McGough to return the favor and more.

Holman was last in line and escaped the initial crushing flail. When a zombie sent Holman's pistol sailing, the seaman had but one thought—run like hell.

He ran for his life, arms pumping side to side, into the potential safety of the room that housed the top portion of the ship's reciprocating engines. Holman's labored breathing might have echoed in the machine room had the reciprocating engines not been so deafening, a steady drone of whirring and pumping that turned *Titanic*'s triple screws. He nearly ran headlong into the room's far wall and panicked, realizing he'd rushed to a dead end. So he spun back the way he came in search of a different escape route.

Ahead, at the edge of the reciprocating room, Holman saw a stairwell that might offer escape. But he never set foot on the stairs or even heard the moan.

24

Zombies in their night clothes and dressing gowns continued to pour forth from cabin doors and filled the foyer. Often two and three emerged from a single room. The numbers were skewed far in the monsters' favor. Andrews shakily raised his Webley pistol. "Stop or I'll shoot again!" he cried. The zombies moaned at his shouts and lumbered toward Andrews as if he'd extended an invitation.

Smith was undaunted. He stepped in front of Andrews and gracefully beheaded two zombies with short, powerful strokes. "Steady, Mr. Andrews," he cautioned. "We'll be done if we lose our heads."

Andrews aimed true, let out a breath slowly, and squeezed the trigger. A zombie's head exploded, its body flying backward and knocking over several more.

Behind them, Weiss grimaced as he used his knife-stick to fight off two men in tattered shirts, working the riddle in his mind all the while. *Had the Kaiser's man somehow slipped the Toxic into the ship's water supply?* While not impossible, it was not probable. The *Titanic's* fresh water tanks were enormous. Even the Toxic would likely become diluted in such a volume, and Weiss was unsure whether the infection could survive such conditions. But somehow, the disease was spreading faster than he'd imagined possible.

Leaving Smith's side, Andrews fought his way toward the edge of the foyer near the first watertight door. He managed to properly unload his gun into the skulls of several would-be attackers, one of whom was close enough to swipe the bowler hat from his head. At last, he reached one of the doors he'd described on the ship's first night. Andrews turned to see that Weiss was still some twenty yards behind, and surrounded.

Andrews aimed his gun at a ghoul near Weiss, but the hammer stopped cold. It was jammed! "Can you make it to me, Mr. Weiss?" yelled Andrews. "My gun's no good, but I can shut this door and confine the zombies behind it!"

"Excellent, Mr. Andrews," said Smith. "I'm ordering you to hold that door." Smith waded deeper into the pack of zombies to open an avenue of escape for the scientist. "Mr. Weiss! Fight your way to me!" The captain struck down more creatures with a display of swordsmanship that left the German awestruck, each thrust and slash in tempo. "Behind you, Mr. Weiss," cautioned the captain.

Weiss spun, fending off a portly zombie in a ragged robe. He jabbed the ponderous monster in the thigh so that it stumbled to the ground, and then put the blade through the thing's neck. *You can do this*, thought Weiss. *Take the fight to your adversary. Put your fear aside.*

"Perfect, your weapon serves you well. Jab them in the head when possible," Smith instructed. "Now, sir, let's get back to back and return to Mr. Andrews." The two men quickly moved tight together. "From here we dance, Mr. Weiss. I will lead."

Smith began moving in a clockwise pattern and when Weiss didn't immediately follow, the captain ordered, "Stay with me now, it's back to back all the way."

Weiss saw the strategy: Their synchronized movement formed a thrusting, spinning dervish of sorts, with Smith's rapier surgically cutting a path toward the door while Weiss protected the captain's back, constantly stabbing as the fiends grabbed at them from all sides. The rotating motion ensured Smith and Weiss could not be assaulted from the rear and were always shifting among their opponents. The crudity of the zombies' approach aided Smith and Weiss greatly.

Soon they broke through. Smith stopped the circular motion and yelled, "Go, Mr. Weiss!"

Weiss ran, joining Andrews on the other side of the watertight door.

"Now, Mr. Andrews!" ordered the captain. Andrews began lowering the door, as the mob swelled like a river flowing toward the captain. He readied himself to defend the opening till it closed.

"How long will this take to shut?" snapped Weiss.

"Approximately twenty-five seconds," said Andrews.

"They'll overpower the captain by then!"

"These demons," growled Smith, "will do no such thing." He seemed to be somewhere else while unleashing a brutal torrent of lightning-fast, slashing thrusts that sent limbs and heads flying like they were spit out of a tornado.

"Now, Captain Smith," Andrews yelled. Smith turned and slid under the door as it closed the last three feet to the floor.

Weiss and Andrews were speechless at the fury of Captain Smith's final assault. Smith bent over, catching his breath, but otherwise he had emerged without a scratch. Andrews exclaimed, "The beasts couldn't get at you, sir. They couldn't even lay a hand on you! Your skills as a swordsman are simply extraordinary!"

"Let's hope," puffed Smith, his chest heaving, "that they won't be put to the test again."

25

"Here's your gun, Thomas," said Captain Smith, handing the revolver back to Andrews. "I don't expect she'll misfire again."

It had been a long time since Smith handled a pistol, much less repaired one, but after twenty minutes of frustration his knowledge of firearms slowly returned. Once he got the action apart and cleared the jam, the gun went back together much more quickly than it had disassembled.

Weiss had stood guard with his knife-stick as time ticked away, but there had been no immediate threat. Perhaps his fear about the disease spreading throughout the ship was unwarranted. Was it too much to hope that the infection was contained on the other side of the door? All was not perfect, however; Clench and the others still hadn't returned with the torches.

The zombies beat relentlessly against the foyer side of the watertight door. The metallic clanging was unnerving as it reverberated throughout the long corridor that lay ahead of the men.

Weiss remembered the Subject throwing its body recklessly at the walls of the glass encasement on Brocken Mountain, leading with its shoulders, fists, or elbows, sometimes even with its head, in a crazed effort to free itself. Weiss couldn't decide then or now if the behavior stemmed from a mad desire for living flesh or if the violence was a desperate attempt to escape a horrific fate.

"Good Lord," remarked Andrews. "Those things are awfully anxious to have a go at us."

"Ignore them," said Smith. "Now that your gun's back in order, we can't wait any longer for Clench and the others."

"Agreed. And given the hour, it's awfully quiet," said Weiss. "Could we have trapped all the infected passengers on the other side of that door?"

"There's only one way to find out," said Smith. "We owe it anybody who still might be healthy and hiding to get them to safety. Fan out and check the cabins to see if there's anyone left to save."

Andrews peered around the corner to his left. Cabin doors lined either side of a short corridor off the main hallway, and four similar layouts waited ahead. Andrews took one step toward the nearest cabins and stopped short. "Captain, shouldn't we get you to the bridge? If we run into another murderous bunch, they might finish us. We barely escaped the last one! *Titanic* needs you at the helm."

"Duty comes before my safety or yours. You're givin' into fear," Smith said firmly. "Don't be afraid of the fire, Thomas. Otherwise you'll miss the chance to be forged in it."

Andrews picked up his lantern and straightened his spine. "You're right, of course," he said. He proceeded to the first cabin, turned his passkey in the lock, and slowly pushed the door open.

The cabin was dark. The light from the lantern barely showed that all the sheets were off the beds and chairs were overturned. A bitter stench filled the air. Andrews turned on the overhead light. Nothing but a trunk, a few parasols, and a nice squash racquet or two.

Heavy footsteps in the corridor outside caused Andrews to jump. He drew his gun and rushed back outside the cabin, joining Weiss and the captain as a distinguished-looking man dressed in a tailored suit and hat ran at them with a fire ax. Smith stepped forward and held up a hand. "Down with your weapon, man. You've nothing to fear from us."

The gentleman, panting and red-faced, stopped ten feet in front of the captain, dropped the ax entirely, and doubled over. His hands braced his knees as he tried to catch his breath. "You're . . . not . . . one of them?"

Neither the captain nor Andrews replied, as Weiss looked the man over carefully. The German found no outward signs of infection and nodded his approval to the captain.

"I'm Captain Edward J. Smith. And you're under my protection now."

"Obliged," the gentleman managed through labored breaths. He spoke with a refined British accent and seemed the type of passenger Mr. Ismay worked hard to court. His dark hair was fashionably slicked back and his thin mustache impeccable. "Hargraves, Oliver Hargraves. Couldn't sleep so I came down here for a bit of early morning exploring. I've been fighting for my life ever since. What the bloody hell is happening on this ship?"

Weiss's heart sank at the news that the infection wasn't contained after all. "There's been an outbreak . . ."

"An outbreak? A disease? The blokes I saw were eating other passengers! I fended the beasts off with this fire ax! What kind of disease—"

"The worst kind," interrupted the captain. "As you've seen for yourself, it turns men into demons. What some have called zombies. We're assessing the situation so we can bring things under control. Stick with us. We'll see you out of this area shortly."

"*Assessing* the situation?" Hargraves said in shock. "There's nothing to assess. We have to get off this damn boat as soon as—"

The sound of a door banging against a wall thirty feet down the hall interrupted their conversation. The sound of low deep moans filled the corridor, quickly followed by the sight of stiffened human forms. Another door banged open, and a second crowd emerged.

Weiss understood in a flash. The sickened passengers, instead of remaining nauseous in their cabins, must have fled for the lavatories, which were more dignified places to deal with their maladies. However, as their transformations worsened, they never returned to their rooms. When newly sickened passengers arrived in each lavatory, they must have delivered themselves into the waiting arms and mouths of those who were already fully diseased. Now a steady stream of male-zombies staggered forth from one side, while female-zombies emerged from the other.

Smith motioned Hargraves to move behind him. The gentleman raised his ax just the same. Andrews drew his gun and pointed it down the hall.

"Mr. Andrews," said Smith as he lunged forward to meet the first of their attackers, "you'll take care not to shoot us."

Smith removed the head of the first drooling ghoul, and then the rapier leaped and sliced, separating sinew and bone. "These demons are slow as tortoises," said Smith. "But my God, their numbers!"

Weiss flanked him, running his stick-blade right between the red eyes of a foul-mouthed zombie dressed for church, in an expensive suit and silk tie. The German withdrew the blade quickly and jabbed it through the neck of a second female demon in a prim, floor-length ivory dress. With a start, Weiss realized that it must indeed be Sunday morning, though he had lost all track of time. *Have I unleashed Armageddon?* Weiss punched through a third zombie's forehead with his blade. *I set this in motion. God help me, I won't let it get off this ship.*

Captain Smith dispatched monster after monster. When he wasn't removing heads with short, powerful strokes, the captain was punching through skulls, using his glove and the rapier's pommel as protection for his hand.

A massive bearded zombie, missing a shirt and oozing sickness from sores on his back and neck, managed to grab Weiss as the scientist was withdrawing his blade from a fallen foe. The creature threw Weiss into the wall, hard enough to dislodge an electrical junction box.

Weiss fell to the floor grabbing his right shoulder, now dislocated. His cane lay to the side. Blinding pain shot through Weiss as he reached for his weapon.

An anguished moan from above rattled in his ears. Weiss realized he couldn't grab the cane, and looked up in terror. The zombie's bearded maw was about to rip open his head.

26

"Mr. Hargraves!" shouted Captain Smith, occupied with three approaching members of the zombie horde. "Please assist Mr. Weiss!"

Hargraves turned and kicked at the bearded zombie descending upon the scientist. As the zombie tumbled, Hargraves swung his fire ax, severing the beast's head mere inches from Weiss's own.

"Well done," shouted Smith.

"I'm in your debt, Mr. Hargraves," said Weiss, grimacing at the pain in his shoulder as he moved gingerly to his feet.

Weiss took in the scene as Hargraves returned to the captain's side. They were badly outnumbered in the narrow hallway. Side corridors offered no escape, only more cabins and dead ends. Some two dozen monsters remained, with no telling how much more wickedness yet to appear from the passenger rooms or adjacent hallways.

Just then, a cabin door opened near Captain Smith. An elderly woman in a nightgown peeked out, apparently awakened by all the clatter. When she saw the carnage, she screamed a stream of hysterical Italian. Half a dozen zombies turned toward her.

"Inside and lock your door!" shouted Captain Smith, slicing down two beasts from behind, but not before one had pressed the woman back inside her cabin. Another flung the door wide, and more followed the scent of healthy flesh. The woman's screams soon faded to silence beneath the gruesome sounds of monsters gnawing her apart.

"There's another watertight door ahead—we could slam it like before!" shouted Andrews. He had exhausted his ammunition and was reduced to swinging his lantern wildly. One swing made solid contact with a ghoul's cheekbone, sending a mass of decomposing flesh to the floor.

One zombie, a woman in a black shawl now living her own funeral, came for Smith. Out of breath and exhausted, he smote the unseemly wretch with his sword, ending its misery. At the same instant, the damaged junction box exploded, sending sparks into the air. The windowless corridor descended into darkness as all the electric lights went out on Deck Z.

"Bloody hell!" shouted the captain, wielding his sword blindly in front of him. With painful slowness, his eyes adjusted to the dark. The only sources of illumination were two flickering lanterns that Mr. Andrews had abandoned on the corridor floor. To Weiss, the monsters seemed to grow in the low, murky lantern light, casting long shadows that hung over the men like a gang of *Brockengespensts*.

"Close ranks!" cried the captain. All would be doomed if they did not fight together in the black. Then he noticed one of the lanterns bouncing away down a side corridor.

"Stand and fight, man! That's an order!" he yelled, but Andrews kept running. "The man isn't a sailor or a soldier," Smith shouted over to Weiss, "but I never imagined him a coward!"

Weiss and Hargraves found their way to the captain, forming a crude wedge. Hargraves battled bravely with his ax, while Weiss struggled to fight left-handed, clumsily wielding the knife-stick. His dislocated right shoulder alternately pulsed with piercing pain, then dull aching. Sensing weakness, another group of monsters down the hall started for Weiss. In the dim light, their dull nightgowns and caps matched their lifeless expressions.

Smith continued to carve his way through undead fiends, one after another, inching their group ever closer to the next watertight door. At the captain's back Hargraves found it wasn't always easy to swing an ax in such close quarters, and the gentleman made do with the butt of the handle more than once. Meanwhile, Weiss fought purely on guts. He punched his heavy cane up and through the neck of a tall, gruesome beast in a topcoat. Sickly gurgling sounds escaped the gape in its throat as Weiss twisted the blade, turning his own body to avoid the black slime that leached from the wound.

The pain in Weiss's shoulder was becoming intolerable. The stick felt heavy and awkward. In a moment of inattention, Weiss missed the sweeping arm of a furious zombie-steward, who sent the German tumbling to the floor again.

Behind the trio, a brilliant burst of light flooded the hall. The men blinked at the brightness as the intense blue flame caught the zombies' attention, and they hesitated. Andrews had returned, squash racquet in one hand, burning torch in the other. Crouching to his knees, Andrews used his torch to spark a squash ball, yelling, "Hit the decks!"

As soon as the ball caught flame, he bounced it off the ground, and swung the racquet hard. The flaming orb flashed through the darkness and struck the savage threatening Weiss in the side of the head. The ball exploded on contact and engulfed the monster in a bright blue blaze. The thing let loose with a horrible, piercing shriek and flailed its arms in an inept attempt to extinguish the flames. The fiery zombie lurched backward, spreading the flames to the stained nightshirts and finery of others.

Weiss crawled from the fiery chaos and rejoined Hargraves and Smith, while Andrews employed his racquet to send two more fireballs hissing down the corridor, each delivering a shot of hellfire.

"I slit the squash balls and filled them with kerosene," shouted Andrews. "Racquet strings for fuses!"

"Ingenious!" shouted Smith.

The men retreated down the hall to help Andrews ignite more squash balls, lobbing them in the air for him to launch furiously at their attackers. The improvised projectiles exploded one by one, blasting the beasts back down the corridor. The flames didn't seem to pain the zombies exactly, but they burned just the same as small explosions knocked the clumsy things off their feet.

"Well played, sir," said Hargraves, his face lit orange from the explosions.

Andrews had cleared a path through the burning zombies to the watertight door, but the passage was not likely to stay open for long. The pile of projectiles had dwindled to almost nothing. Andrews and Smith gathered the last ball-bomb and the remaining lantern, with Hargraves and Weiss following. All four men hurried through flames and sickly black smoke. Weiss had hoped he would never again have to smell the revolting stench of burning putrefied flesh.

The zombies mindlessly grabbed at the men's legs as they passed, but Smith cut the way through like an explorer clearing jungle brush with his machete.

"Stay with us now, Mr. Weiss," shouted Smith. "We're nearly to the watertight door."

"I will," Weiss burbled, delirious from pain and nausea.

"Look there, Captain," warned Andrews. Ahead, on the other side of the watertight door, more zombies could be seen in the gloom, stumbling awkwardly in the hallway, drawn by the light of the fire. Shutting the door would be no protection after all.

"Shall we set the whole corridor ablaze?" asked Hargraves.

"Given the condition of our friend Mr. Weiss," said Andrews, "I have a more practical idea." Andrews doused his lantern. "Follow me."

27

Twenty-one-year-old Harold Bride earned two dollars a week as a Marconi man, but he would have done the job for half that amount. A quiet boy in school, Bride dreamed of being a wireless operator. Secret messages flying through the air! And only the magical Marconi men could pluck them from the ether.

His parents didn't have much money, so Bride worked to put himself through training. Only eight months after completing his studies, Bride was on *Titanic*. He imagined the voyage might bring messages of international import or intrigue from presidents and kings, but the actual communications had been rather mundane thus far—mostly of the "I trust you're having a delightful trip" variety.

So it was with a secret thrill that Harold Bride received a message from the *Baltic,* a liner making its way eastward from New York to Liverpool:

Greek steamer Athenia reports passing icebergs and large quantities of field ice today in latitude 41° 51'N, longitude 49° 52'W. Wish you and Titanic all success. Commander.

For Bride, a warning of icebergs topped his personal list of "most compelling messages received so far." Bride immediately shared the message with Jack Phillips, *Titanic*'s senior wireless operator.

"You know the policy," said Phillips, more jaded about such missives after five years at sea. "Passenger messages first. They're payin' the bills, ain't they?"

Bride acquiesced, but that didn't mean he agreed. Surely reports of field ice were more important than inquiries about the accommodations or Great-Aunt Helen's health. Bride excused himself, message in pocket, and headed down the narrow passageway that connected the Marconi room to the officers' quarters and wheelhouse.

On the bridge, Mr. Henry Tingle Wilde was in command, though his head was elsewhere. He stared out at the black waters as the ship pushed ahead at top speed. It was only because of a last-minute change of orders that Wilde was even on *Titanic*. He had been serving as chief officer of *Olympic* only days before receiving this surprise assignment, and he'd had misgivings from the start.

There was something peculiar, even sinister about the new liner. *I don't like this ship*, Wilde wrote to his sister at the start of the voyage. *I have a queer feeling about it.* But even the surest of hunches couldn't have foreseen a cannibalistic plague belowdecks. Would *Titanic* ever reach shore? *One thing's certain*, Wilde promised himself, *I will never sail on* Titanic *again.*

"I've a message from *Baltic*, a warning of ice ahead!"

Bride was nearly out of breath, more from excitement than exertion. Lost in his thoughts, Wilde barely heard the young radio man.

"Sir?" said Bride, offering the message. "A message from *Baltic*? I believe it's urgent."

"Ice, yes, ice ahead," said Wilde. *And where was Captain Smith? Why hadn't he called the bridge yet?*

Bride cleared his throat to remind the chief officer of his presence. Wilde shook free from his reverie and said, "We'll be sure to alert the men in the crow's nest. Thank you for your diligence. Such warnings are routine at this time of year. A ship this size has little to fear from ice."

Bride hadn't sailed on many ships, but he knew when he was being dismissed. He saluted Mr. Wilde and set off in search of someone who might take the threat more seriously: Captain E. J. Smith himself.

The captain proved a hard man to find. The young man first looked in the captain's quarters, then the first-class dining saloon, but no one had seen the captain for many hours. Bride needed to return to the Marconi room very soon—his absence had extended well beyond the ordinary breaks he and Phillips allowed one another. Bride hurried down the open boat deck, imagining where a sea captain might be when not commanding his ship. Then the Marconi operator spotted J. Bruce Ismay speaking to a man with a chiseled face and two elegant ladies in deck chairs, which were turned to take advantage of the high sun.

"Mr. Ismay!" Bride exclaimed. "Excuse the interruption, but have you seen the captain? He's not on the bridge."

Ismay looked Bride up and down, not placing him despite the White Star uniform.

"Harold Bride, sir. Radio operator," said Bride, answering Ismay's unspoken question. "I have an urgent message for the captain."

Not in front of Kaufmann, thought Ismay, who had ten lies at the ready to explain the captain's mysterious whereabouts. "The captain," he said, smiling easily, "is attending to some private business at the moment. I'll take the message and personally make sure he receives it at the first opportunity."

"It's a message from the *Baltic*, Mr. Ismay," said Bride, handing over the paper on which he'd typed out the wire.

Ismay squinted at the type, then patted his pockets in an unsuccessful search for his reading spectacles. He nodded for Bride's help. The Marconi man looked uncomfortably at the listening passengers: "A warning of ice ahead, sir."

Marian Thayer sat forward in her deck chair, putting one hand to her mouth and reaching over with the other to touch her friend, Emily Ryerson. "Ice!" Thayer exclaimed. "Are we in danger?"

"Danger?" laughed Ismay, shaking his head. He held up Bride's message to passengers strolling past on their afternoon walks. "Ice! Cubes of ice up ahead! Alert the stewards! Man the Punch Romaine!"

To Bride's chagrin, the women giggled demurely. He was learning an important lesson: Experienced seamen apparently were used to receiving ice warnings. His concern only betrayed his inexperience.

"Imagine the fight, Mr. Kaufmann!" exclaimed Ismay. "In one corner, we have some ice! In the other, *sixty-six thousand pounds* of the world's mightiest steel! I'm no betting man, but if I were, you can be certain where my money would be."

"I'd need more information to make that bet," said Kaufmann. "For instance, I'd love to hear more about the private business keeping your captain from his command. Could it be related to the reason I'm not allowed belowdecks?"

Bride bowed his head and made to excuse himself. "I'm sorry, Mr. Ismay. I shouldn't have bothered you."

"You did the right thing," said Ismay, slapping Bride on the shoulder and ignoring Kaufmann. "You've alerted the officers on the bridge, correct?" When Bride nodded, Ismay continued, "Very responsible. I'll make sure the captain receives this message as soon as his business is finished."

"Yes, sir," said Bride, eager to take his leave. "Thank you, sir."

Ismay smiled at the ladies, folded the message, and secreted it away in his breast pocket. He walked Bride a few steps down the deck and gave him a long, direct look. "Send a wire for me to the White Star offices in New York, and keep it confidential, understand?"

"Certainly, sir," said Bride, hurriedly fishing for a pencil stub and scrap of paper from his pocket. "What is the message?"

"Due to arrive earlier than expected. Stop. Monday night. Stop. Extra security necessary for disembarkation. Stop. Crowds could be dangerous. Stop. Be prepared for all contingencies. Stop."

20

In the dark, with only the illumination of the dying flames in the corridor behind as a guide, Andrews quickly led the men down a side hall and into a storage room. They stumbled inside and locked the door. "Hopefully," Andrews whispered in the dark, "the zombies won't have seen our escape. If we remain quiet, the locked door should dissuade any that wander this way, at least until we can get you right, Mr. Weiss."

Andrews relit his lantern with his pocket lighter. The men were surrounded by splintered crates full of potatoes stacked nearly to the ceiling. At the sudden light, a few rats skittered out of sight underneath the wooden pallets that kept the crates off the floor. An earthy, damp smell hung heavy in the humid room.

Weiss slumped to the floor and Smith propped the scientist up against the crates. He tried to put on a brave face but winced at the slightest contact with his damaged shoulder. Weiss's arm hung at an odd angle, and he seemed on the verge of passing out.

"Mr. Hargraves, you don't happen to have anything that could put a man at ease, do you?" the captain asked. "A flask, perhaps?"

"I wish I did," the gentleman replied. "We could all use a slug of medicine right now."

Moaning sounds outside the storage room grew louder. Andrews piled heavy potato crates against the locked door as an extra precaution. He looked pale as an onion in the dim, flickering light. "Our kerosene supply is low," he warned. "Should I extinguish the lantern so we can conserve its fuel for more tactical purposes?"

"In a moment," said Smith. "I have some work to do first. All right then, Mr. Weiss. Try to breathe." The captain knelt at Weiss's side, bending the scientist's elbow at a ninety-degree angle so Weiss's clenched fist rested against his stomach. Weiss groaned in agony. "Please . . . stop . . ."

"I know what I'm doing, Mr. Weiss."

Smith took a few deep breaths to focus. As Weiss grunted in pain, memories arose that Smith preferred not to revisit, memories of war that he had taken to the sea to forget. Smith had never fought zombies before, but he'd seen the carnage of combat. For a moment he was back on a bloody battlefield, mending a man who had been one of his closest friends. Despite Smith's best efforts, his friend did not survive.

Edward Smith had been a young man then, a cavalryman in the British Army and foolishly cavalier about many things: Britain's place in the world, his own abilities as a soldier, a future he saw as assured. Smith was a proud member of the Guides, elite warriors assigned to protect the British Consulate in Afghanistan.

Kabul.

There had been a treaty in place, a promise of peace. Vain men with far more authority than Smith grossly overestimated the protection that piece of parchment and the British Army's reputation provided. To this day, Smith couldn't believe no one saw the uprising coming, himself included. When thousands of angry Afghan soldiers pounded on the doors of the consulate, only four Brits and sixty-odd Indian soldiers were inside to defend it.

The Guides should have been overwhelmed immediately. But they were students of their commander, Major Pierre Louis Napoleon Cavagnari. He was Italian by birth but British where it counted, Smith always believed. The major was a great leader of men and an even greater teacher of the proper art of sword fighting.

Smith and the other soldiers had learned well. Though numbering fewer than seventy, they killed at least six hundred Afghan soldiers before being overrun. Once the Guides exhausted their ammunition, they charged forth from the consulate's protective walls and fought with bayonets and swords. It was a bloody nightmare not unlike what Smith had just relived on Deck Z—missing limbs, decapitated heads, and the horror all desperate battles bring.

Many times in the ensuing years Smith wished he'd perished with his brothers. Bloody and finally beaten, he and the others had been left to die. He'd crawled among the dying men—trying desperately to bandage wounds, tie tourniquets, cover the torn ends of dismembered body parts. All for naught. It was his destiny to be Britain's sole survivor of the battle at Kabul.

Smith's own weapon had been a rapier, an agile sword that had served him well. Some years later, Smith found a blacksmith who fashioned a new blade. It resembled a rapier but incorporated elements of the long sword—light, yet strong, a blade that could slice as well as stab. He named it *Kabul* to remember the lesson of the day he was left for dead: Arrogance diminishes wisdom.

"Aaaaaaargh!" cried Weiss. Captain Smith forcefully turned the scientist's fist, guiding the shoulder back into its proper place with a hard thrust and an audible *pop*. Weiss's eyes went wide, then shut tight. He clutched his shoulder, now back where it rightly belonged.

"Feel better?" asked Smith.

"I . . . yes," said Weiss, gingerly rotating his right arm to test his shoulder. "Still sore, but everything seems back in working order."

"A doctor couldn't have done better, Captain," said Hargraves.

"Not even O'Loughlin himself," agreed Andrews. "It does not bode well that we've still had no sign of him."

"No time to worry about O'Loughlin now," said Smith, who got to his feet. "Mr. Weiss, if you're strong enough to continue, we have a ship to save."

Just then, a quiet *creak* sounded from behind the pile of crates. Andrews and Hargraves froze. Smith slipped Kabul from its sheath as the stack wavered slightly.

They were not alone.

"Show yourself, demon!" bellowed Smith, raising Kabul high above his head.

A small sob emerged from the darkness behind the stack of crates. Andrews held a hand up, forestalling Smith's blow. He pulled away a carton, as more rats scurried from their hiding places. Shivering in the corner, too frightened to speak, was a little girl.

"Lou," Weiss choked. "Dear God, *Louise!*"

"Answer my call next time, girl," growled Captain Smith, "unless you want your bloody head cut off."

Andrews pulled Lou forward. She immediately collapsed to the floor and wrapped her arms around her knees, rocking to and fro as if to calm horrific visions threatening to destroy her from the inside.

"Louise," said Weiss, lifting her head gently. "Look at me."

Lou looked up till dim awareness crept back into her eyes. "Mr. Nosworthy?"

The German examined her for signs of sickness, then allowed himself a weak smile. Her eyes were dark, sunken, and red from crying, but there was no evidence of black contagion in her nose or mouth. "Actually, my name is Theodor Weiss," admitted the scientist. "Call me Mr. Weiss."

"Mr. Weiss?" Lou repeated vaguely, emerging from her shock.

"Where's your family?" Hargraves asked.

Lou flinched. "Ain't got none, not no more."

Though Weiss dreaded bearing the news, Lou deserved to hear the truth about the woman who seemed so determined to put her on a better path in America. "I have seen your mother . . ."

"I don't got no mother!" hollered Lou. "She's gone, just like all the others! They're all gone, the cleaning woman, them boys—they're all changed!" She angrily wiped more tears from her dirty cheeks.

The men were awkwardly silent—consoling an anguished child was a talent none of them possessed. No matter; Lou was in no mood to be soothed. The only sound was the moaning of the zombies, growing louder and nearer than ever. Some even scratched or clawed the door outside. The party had been found.

"I need me a gun," she said flatly. "I'll kill those things that did that to my mum." A rat ran between her legs, and she unleashed a savage kick at the rodent, which flew into the wall with a crack, then lay twitching on the floor.

"Damned rats," said Andrews. "They spread like the plague."

"Rats," said Weiss softly. Then, "That's it! That's the answer."

"Explain yourself, man," said Smith.

"I've been thinking of this the wrong way. I assumed the infection must be spreading person to person, but there's too many of them. It doesn't make sense. Each zombie we've encountered would have had to infect twenty others. There just hasn't been time."

"Indeed," agreed Smith. "We came hoping for a handful, and yet it's as if everyone was infected all at once."

Weiss gestured animatedly as he pieced together the puzzle. "All along I've thought the Kaiser's man infected the cook. That's wrong."

"He infected a rat," concluded Hargraves.

"He didn't want to infect the ship—he was testing my claim that the vial contained cyanide! Even if the rat didn't survive, the disease would be passed along by the fleas on its hide. Rat fleas infected the cook! That's how the infection is spreading so virulently!"

The captain stroked his beard. "Mr. Andrews is unfortunately correct. You cannot completely contain rats on any ship, but they are mainly found where the food is stored. That means from this deck on down. If the vermin have spread this to the men firing the boilers, *Titanic* will truly be dead in the water."

Andrews said soberly, "We must close every one of the watertight doors from Deck Z to the bottom of the ship. There's not a monster or a rat that can get through that steel."

"Surely you're not suggesting we trap ourselves down here with the monsters," stammered Hargraves.

"Closing the doors will only prevent the zombies and rats from moving forward and aft," explained Andrews. "That should confine the menace on any given deck. Some of the hatches and stairwells are open, but protected by our armed guards. Obviously, they will let us pass."

"That's the best option, but we'll drop if we try to fight our way from one watertight door to the next," said Smith. "We'll need to make our way back to the bridge and the master door switches."

"It sounds as if we'll have to battle more monsters no matter which way we go," sighed Hargraves.

"I'll fight," offered Lou. "God help me, I'll fight!"

"Hold on," said Andrews. "Perhaps there's a better way." He walked to the rear of the room with the lantern, revealing a second door. He put his ear against it and smiled. "We don't need to get all the way to the bridge. There aren't many phones on the passenger decks; they're mostly in the working areas. We just need to get to the nearest one so the captain can contact the bridge—"

"And slam the barriers in a blink," Smith finished. "A sound plan, Thomas."

Andrews eyed them all. "I hate to suggest going down, but the closest phone I know of from here is in the baker's shop, which should be just below on Deck F."

"Chart us a path," Smith declared.

The group eyed the locked door, and for a long moment they listened to the sounds of the zombie horde scraping fruitlessly at the handle outside. "Those mindless things are focused on the door we came through, but no one's on this side," he said. "There's stairs just outside that lead straight down to Deck F."

Weiss retracted his blade so he could use the stick for support. He put a hand around Lou's shoulder. "Let's get you to America."

29

"Everyone ready?" Andrews asked.

The others nodded, Andrews extinguished the lantern, and the room went pitch-black.

"Be bloody silent from here out," whispered the captain. Slowly, Andrews turned the knob and pushed the door open. Moans could be heard farther down the dank hall and around the corner, but the path to the stairs was clear—fifteen feet away to the right. Andrews held the door as Smith, Lou, Hargraves, and finally Weiss passed silently over to the shadowy stairwell and descended away from Deck Z.

Andrews brought up the rear. As his eyes strained to adjust to the dark, his shoulder collided with the edge of the stairwell's metal Bostwick folding gate. A dreadful metallic *clang* reverberated through the hallways. Moans rose and quickened, followed by the whisper of shuffling feet.

"Come on now!" said the captain from below in the dark.

"I can hold them off!" returned Andrews. "Wait for me at the landing."

Andrews quickly set down the kerosene lantern and unfolded the metal gate, stretching it tight across the top of the stairwell. He reached for the padlock, but it wasn't hanging from its usual spot on the latch.

Andrews fell to his hands and knees and swept the ground blindly in the dark. *Where was the damned lock?* Then he jumped in fright as the gate rattled: three monsters stood above him, putrefied hands wrapped around the gate. When it did not move, they growled in rage and shook the bars with a ravenous fury, not realizing the metal barrier opened by sliding sideways.

A tiny girl still in pin-curls, but with a black-stained face devoid of life, reached through a space in the folding gate and got hold of Andrews's pant leg, yanking hard. The architect kicked at the child, breaking her grip. He readjusted his trousers, and that gave him an idea.

He removed his leather belt and looped it through the folding gate and its metal frame. The creatures bellowed, trying to reach him through the gate's openings. One grabbed his jacketed arm, but Andrews jerked backward, slamming the zombie into the steel webbing, and the fiend let go. Finally, Andrews cinched a knot he hoped would secure the gate for at least a short time and then retrieved his lantern.

"Yaaaargh!" Andrews bellowed at the creatures and made his escape down the stairwell. *That felt good*, he thought.

Power still functioned on Deck F, and the corridor blazed with light and the rumbling of the ship's turbines. Weiss recognized their location immediately and raced off without a word to the laundry closet where he had been tortured by the Agent. In a moment, Weiss returned with an armful of pillowcases as Andrews rejoined them.

"These will protect our faces," Weiss explained. "Against both fleas and mucus."

Captain Smith caught on and used his penknife to cut eye slits in the linens.

Weiss turned to Lou. "I found these for you." He held up a pair of trousers. "We'll need to cuff them, but they should protect your legs."

"Thanks," said Lou. She shimmied them up under her skirt. "Better for running, that's for sure." She looked up and laughed. "We look like a bunch of train robbers!"

"Where to now, Mr. Andrews?" asked Captain Smith.

"Let me see," Andrews said. "The bakery is past the turbine casing, stewards' quarters, and near more stairwells that should serve as escape routes if we need them. Follow me."

The group trotted swiftly and silently, without speaking. Behind several doors they heard anguished moans, but no cries for help. No one raised the possibility of stopping to investigate any of the noises. They knew what made the sounds, and it only spurred them on.

They remained unchallenged until they turned the final corner to the bakery, then their luck gave out. A collection of zombies in black-stained kitchen uniforms appeared to be feeding on some hidden form in the doorway of the third-class galley. Lou screamed, and every zombie looked up.

The group froze for a moment, then Andrews reached for the final kerosene-filled squash ball. Smith grabbed his arm. "Not now, man," Smith said. "The numbers don't warrant it. Save it for when we really need it."

Weiss snapped the blade on his walking stick into position. "Are we to stand and fight, Captain?" asked Weiss.

"Blimey," said Lou, momentarily forgetting her terror. "I could do with one of those."

Captain Smith addressed Weiss. "No, not this time. The noise will only attract others, and I don't want to get surrounded again. Mr. Andrews, plot us an alternate route. Is there another phone?"

"None unless we travel down another deck," said Andrews. "Our best bet is still to find another way to this . . ."

Seven of the zombies now neared the party.

"Be fast about it, man," urged Hargraves.

Andrews started running back the way they had come, then made a hard left. The others followed, needing no more prompting. "There's a back way into the bakery," Andrews called. "But I'm not certain this route will be any easier."

Guarding their rear, Captain Smith unsheathed Kabul and looked back. The zombies were pursuing, but they were falling farther behind. Perhaps speed and stealth might win the day where brute force failed.

Andrews turned the corner and stopped abruptly before an ascending flight of stairs. A balding zombie in a matted brown vest fell down the steps head-first and landed on his bloated stomach.

Lou ran to the front of the group and pulled her foot back to kick the thing, but Weiss stopped her just in time. "Don't touch them, Lou!" he shouted.

The zombie rolled over, and as it did, Weiss thrust his bladed walking stick into its gaping mouth. The weapon rammed clean out the back side of its head, stopping the monster's moans immediately. The rotting body went limp. Weiss looked up the stairwell to see a dozen or more zombies crowded at the top, who moaned louder at the sight of him and awkwardly began testing the steps down.

"It's no good, Andrews," Weiss announced, pointing up the stairs.

Captain Smith felt his frustrations and exhaustion getting the better of him. "Andrews, where in the hell are you taking us?"

"Stewards' quarters, that way," he responded. "We'll work our way through them back to the bakery."

Hargraves peeked back down the main corridor as their original attackers closed the gap. "Those others are nearly on us now. We can't get anywhere without them following us."

"I can help," Lou cried. She ran through an open door into a dry goods storage area.

"Lou!" Weiss exclaimed. "What are you doing?"

She returned, proudly hoisting two five-pound bags of flour in her arms. "Got the switch at school for throwing one of these, I did. She'll make a cloud all right." Lou handed one to Hargraves, who grinned at the girl's resourcefulness.

"Now, Mr. Hargraves!" Lou yelled. They threw their bags of flour high in the air, and the bags burst upon impact, filling the corridor with a white opaque cloud. As the blinded zombies floundered, bumping into the walls and each other, Andrews led the others down a jog to the left, and all five of the party slipped into the stewards' quarters.

Andrews quickly locked the door behind them. The group stood anxiously in the dark. The room was filled with a pained clamor, and the party steeled themselves for an imminent attack.

It never happened, as the five went unnoticed. The suffering continued uninterrupted from around the room, gurgling and gasping, the spitting sounds of drowning men. How many were there? Lou could not guess. But it was worse than listening to the zombie moans outside. She was listening to people die.

"No one dare reach for a light," muttered Captain Smith in a voice too quiet to be called a whisper. "This is a hornet's nest. Don't stir it."

With a *thump*, a body hit the floor and a man howled in anguish. Writhing on the ground and ripping at his clothing, the man lay mere feet away from where the party stood. Smith knew the men who bunked in this room—many were stewards who had served him on *Olympic, Baltic,* and other White Star ships. They were good men, dedicated to their jobs and to the sea, several with wives and children. They didn't deserve this.

"Hail Mary, full of grace, the Lord is with thee . . ." One of the stewards muttered a rosary punctuated with painful coughs.

"Some faculties remain," Weiss said quietly. "They haven't all changed, not all the way. We might move through unchallenged, but we haven't much time. Mr. Andrews?"

"Yes," returned Andrews in a hush. "The door at the back of the room. We just have to find it."

30

Titanic bandleader Wallace Hartley had been performing on liners for three years. A deeply religious man dating back to his days as a choirboy at Bethel Independent Methodist Chapel in Colne, Hartley had prayed many nights for the opportunity to lead his own band. He realized that dream some years later on the Cunard line of ships, and in 1912 his prayers were answered to the fullest when he was chosen to lead accomplished musicians on the finest ship in the world. But by then his wanderlust was anchored by the overwhelming weight of love.

Shortly before receiving notice from the music agency C. W. & F. N. Black that he had won the job of *Titanic* bandleader, Hartley had proposed to young Miss Maria Robinson, who was everything he hoped to find in a wife—kind, curious, a soprano. *Titanic's* maiden voyage had interrupted preparations for their nuptials, but Maria was never far from Hartley's thoughts, and their wedding day could not come fast enough. Being away from her was the hardest chore his heart had ever endured, yet when he began to feel less than thankful, he sternly reminded himself that God had seen fit to bless him doubly. Hartley was sure his life had been moved by God's steady hand. The Englishman felt an obligation to the Lord to be dutiful, and right now that meant being a good bandleader. Soon, as God saw fit, it would also mean being a good husband.

Hartley turned to face his assembled musicians, still tuning and preparing to play for a boisterous audience of first-class passengers.

George Krins, first violinist and master of the strings section, appeared out of sorts. His eyes darted around the lounge at the wealthy passengers in their finery, arguing with their spouses, complaining about the service, and obsessing about the latest fashions. It was Krins's first tour on a liner—his previous job was playing at the Ritz in London. He was accustomed to audiences waiting in hushed anticipation for the music to begin. The last thing this distracted mob seemed to be interested in was the band.

Hartley had performed for many such audiences. He walked alongside the young violinist. "Mr. Krins," said Hartley in a low voice next to his ear, "I understand that you are used to playing under rather different conditions."

"We could be replaced with a gramophone for all they care," said Krins. "Half of them are unhappy and no one appears interested in anything but his own business. They'll never listen."

"*Titanic* is my third liner," said Hartley, "so you'll have to trust me on this: When we start playing, they'll forget their cares. Nothing is nobler than to use our God-given gifts for such good."

Krins raised a skeptical eyebrow, but he smiled and gave a brief, deferential nod.

Across the room, Charlotte Wardle Cardeza curled a finger and summoned her favorite personal maid. "Miss Anna, go retrieve my bottle of L'Heure Bleue. It is well past the hour for a puff of Guerlain. I believe it's in trunk number nine." Lady Cardeza posed prominently in front of one of the panoramic windows, gazing out at the blue waters of the Atlantic. "Hurry now, I don't want to be beaten to that fragrance by some Luddite from London."

The maid scurried off to fetch the perfume. As another servant stood ready at her side, Lady Cardeza surveyed the room for a social figure of at least equal stature. It had been fifteen minutes since she had been seen with anyone of standing.

She spied her former dinner guest Emil Kaufmann, alone and sipping a martini one window bay over. She hadn't spotted him of late and didn't quite know what to make of the man—a reasonably handsome face and position of some regard but so enigmatic. No matter, she decided. He would have to do.

Lady Cardeza sashayed with practiced elegance across the room, only to trip and stumble halfway to her quarry. Doubtlessly, the five martinis she had earlier consumed accounted for the error. The Lady checked the room furtively to ensure no one of consequence had witnessed the incident. Her wig was akimbo; she artfully adjusted it as if nothing had happened. *You pay a king's ransom for these things*, she thought, *and they never stay on straight.*

"Lady Cardeza," Kaufmann said agreeably. "I'm afraid you could do far better than I for company at the moment."

She batted her eyelids. "Why would you say such a thing, Mr. Kaufmann?"

"I am confronted with a nuisance that apparently cannot be remedied and am feeling quite dour. I never expected to be inconvenienced so, on this, of all ships."

"Do tell, sir. I, too, shall complain at the first opportunity about that horrible rug back there. It has more bumps than a cobblestone street!"

"As well you should complain. What good is it to have the ear of those in power if you're unwilling to bend it from time to time?" Kaufmann's charming smile was a tonic, but not the one Lady Cardeza needed. She snatched another martini from a passing valet's tray.

The gentleman touched Lady Cardeza's hand and nodded discreetly across the room. "Why, there's Mr. Ismay right now."

"It most certainly is," hooted Lady Cardeza. "Let's go have a word with him."

Yet before Lady Cardeza and Kaufmann could reach Ismay, he was confronted by another agitated passenger, George Dunton Widener.

"Bruce," Widener said, his hand wrapped around a glass of whiskey and a fat cigar clenched between his teeth, "my wife would like to take a Turkish bath."

Ismay laughed nervously. "Well, by all means," he said. "I wish I had time for such pleasures myself, but I really must be . . ."

"Your staff won't allow it!" thundered Widener. "Knock some sense into them. She's tried to go ten different times but they won't even let her in the stairwell. Eleanor is beside herself!"

"Mr. Ismay!"

The White Star chairman recognized the shrill, piercing voice of Lady Cardeza. She had that German, Kaufmann, in tow. Ismay winced. *What now?*

"Mr. Ismay," Lady Cardeza puffed, "Mr. Kaufmann and I have bones to pick with you."

"Yes, well, of course, if there's any problem at all I'd like to know straight away." Manners dictated that Ismay address Lady Cardeza first, but he overrode such concerns to concentrate on the competition. "Mr. Kaufmann, what is the trouble?"

"I have business several decks below, but I've been restricted by ship personnel from venturing there," said Kaufmann, jaw clenched tight. "I'd like an explanation."

Widener harrumphed in agreement. "You heard the man, Bruce. Please explain why we're being denied our amenities."

With effort, Ismay pushed his anxieties aside and nodded reassuringly. "I understand and apologize for the inconvenience. Purely unintentional. We're just conducting some routine maintenance. I assure you, it will be finished soon." Ismay snapped his fingers at a waiter, who rushed over with a bottle of champagne. Ismay put his arms around both Kaufmann and Lady Cardeza. "Please accept this with my compliments, and anything else that suits your pleasure for the rest of this evening."

"I had better be able to go about my business soon, Ismay," warned Kaufmann, "or you'll surely hear from me again."

Lady Cardeza brandished the opened bottle. "Thank you for the champagne, Mr. Ismay," she called, pulling Kaufmann away. "But your rugs are still bumpy."

Once they'd gone, Widener spun his cigar. "A *new* ship does routine maintenance?"

"*Especially* a new ship," Ismay said, one tycoon to another. "Think of your own street cars—do new models off the line run to form on the very first day?"

Widener chewed and puffed thoughtfully. "I suppose not. But we're charging people an awful lot of money for you to work out the kinks!"

"Let me set your mind at ease," said Ismay. "I have the ship's designer himself down below making sure everything is in tip-top shape. I expect the baths will be open again within the hour."

"Andrews, eh?" nodded Widener. "Very well then. Send someone to get me when Eleanor has run of the ship again, will you?"

"You can bank on it," said Ismay, silently cursing Smith and the men several decks below. New York could not come fast enough.

Widener turned to leave but stopped as music filled the air. He tilted his ear, listening critically. "These chaps are quite good, Bruce. Quite good."

For once Ismay and Widener agreed on something. They stood shoulder to shoulder, transfixed by the music as Wallace Hartley's bow danced across his violin.

31

"The safest route," whispered Andrews to his huddled group of compatriots, "is along the walls. Let's make our way around the room to the door."

"One of those things is going to grab us," said Lou.

Captain Smith put a callused hand to the girl's mouth. She got the picture. No more talking.

Andrews led the way, back and heels to the wall. The others followed in a line, moving slowly and quietly in the darkness. After turning the first corner without incident, Andrews halted. Ahead, he heard the sound of an infected man banging his head against the wall. He would be blocking their path to the door.

"Go back the other way?" whispered Weiss.

"No. Bunks are back there," Andrews replied. "Bunks full of *them*."

"Then," said Smith, "go over him, Mr. Andrews." He prodded Andrews forward.

Andrews carefully leapt the prone figure, who was none the wiser. Next was Weiss, who thought, *It's not as if I haven't had practice navigating in the dark, yet still* . . . He hesitated, then took a long, tentative step over the thrashing creature. As Weiss raised his back foot, he brushed against the zombie's flailing hand. Weiss bit his lip. The poor creature simply kept throwing his cranium at the wall.

Captain Smith was next and leaped as easily as Andrews, but Lou stopped at the prone figure, afraid to continue.

Hargraves first tried to encourage her, but then he simply slipped his hands beneath the child's armpits and lifted her toward the waiting arms of Captain Smith.

Beneath them, the zombie let loose with a guttural moan. It grabbed at Lou's dangling legs.

"It knows we're here!" she screamed.

Andrews had found the door and was waiting by it. Now he opened it, so they could see their attacker. It was like releasing light into a mausoleum.

"Good God," said Weiss. A dozen bodies littered the room and wailed at the light. Several turned their dead, transformed faces toward the room's human visitors.

The zombie on the floor seized Hargraves's leg. Pitching Lou to Captain Smith, Hargraves kicked down on the fiend till its grip released, then leaped past and through the open door on the heels of the others.

Hargraves slammed the door shut and threw the lock. They were in a small utility room with no other exit, clearly a temporary salvation at best. The room contained only three high-speed fans: two large fans for ventilating the number-one boiler casing and a third that served as an exhaust for the bakery on the other side.

Erratic blows rained down on the other side of the wooden door, which, unlike steel, would not stand up to the monsters' brutality.

"Are we at a dead end?" asked the captain.

"Not exactly!" shouted Andrews, pointing to the back wall. "The phone we need is on the other side of that fan!"

"Where are the controls to stop the damned thing?" Captain Smith said. "Those blades will cut us to pieces."

Andrews shook his head in disbelief as his eyes darted about the room. "I swore the switch was in this utility space," he said. "But it must be on the other side of that wall."

Hargraves and Weiss were both putting their weight against the utility room door, which groaned as more zombies began to throw themselves against it.

"I don't think we've got much time," Lou shouted.

"She's right," said Smith, drawing his rapier again.

Hargraves gestured with his ax as the door rattled behind him. "We can't fight the monsters here. There's no room!"

"That's not what we're going to do," countered Smith. "I'm going to stop the fan with this blade."

"But the fan will snap your sword in half," protested Weiss. "Or mangle it till it's useless. Then where will be—with only my cane and Hargraves's ax?"

A thunderous blast splintered the wood by Weiss's ear.

"She'll hold!" Captain Smith roared as he plunged Kabul into the spinning blades near their center. Sparks flew as Kabul's hardened steel lodged firmly and overpowered the groaning motor. The fan came to a standstill. "Go!" Smith ordered. "Go through now, all of you!"

First Lou and then Andrews and Hargraves worked their way between the fan blades and into the bakery on the other side. Another loud *crack* fractured the wooden door. As pieces fell away, the first zombie shoved its head and arm into the opening. Weiss quickly plunged his knife-stick hard into the creature's head, reducing the zombie to a limp mass that plugged the opening in the partially shattered door. Yet the light and sounds of struggle had drawn all the creatures in the steward's quarters. The zombies raged against the barriers separating them from human flesh. The door cracked further, widening the opening, and hands pushed through and pulled at the now freely splintering wood. Weiss stabbed at the reaching hands in vain.

"They're about to break through," Andrews pleaded from the other side of the fan.

Weiss gave up the door and raced to Smith, who continued to hold his sword firm. Weiss said, "Captain, you first. We can't afford to lose you!"

Weiss took hold of the sword's pommel, bracing it with his good shoulder. With a reluctant nod, the captain relented, releasing Kabul and forcing his aching body through the fan blades, cursing under his breath as they gouged into his ribs.

When he was through, Captain Smith called back to Weiss, "What are you going to do now? The fan will start up the second you remove the blade."

In that instant, the door gave way completely. Zombies spilled through into a heap, with more pushing and shuffling behind them. Weiss wedged his right thigh against a fan blade and yanked out the sword. As the fan slowly, relentlessly began to turn, Weiss plunged his upper torso into the opening and through to the other side, then Captain Smith and Andrews grabbed his jacket and pulled just as a zombie took hold of Weiss's legs trailing behind in the fan. Bracing himself, Captain Smith pulled mightily on the scientist, winning the brief tug-of-war. Weiss was pulled into the bakery. The zombie, who still had hold of Weiss's feet, became stuck halfway through, caught by the frustrated fan blade.

Captain Smith brought Kabul down hard and fast on the zombie's wrists, freeing Weiss's leg from its grasp, then he rained blows on the beast until it was nearly cut in half. The fan blade finished the job, and once unblocked, the fan quickly picked up speed again.

Andrews, Smith, and Lou helped Weiss up off the ground, and everyone retreated to the farthest corner of the bakery away from the exhaust fan. Lacking all self-regard, the zombies tried to climb through, and their fingers, hands, and forearms were efficiently severed. Body parts fell harmlessly on the bakery floor, as black fluid splattered from the fan in all directions.

Captain Smith pulled the pillowcase from his head; the others did the same. "Lock and blockade the front door to this room, Mr. Hargraves. I have a call to make."

32

Is there anyone who doesn't want a photograph with Smith? thought Ismay upon seeing yet another tuxedo-clad passenger lurking outside the bridge. There were several reasons E. J. Smith was known as the "Millionaire's Captain"—one was his willingness to accommodate such requests, which had been piling up in his absence. Ismay anxiously awaited word about the situation below, and passenger distractions were the last thing he needed. However, Ismay knew that one particular traveler would not be producing an Eastman Kodak folding pocket camera. It was Emil Kaufmann, and he had something other than snapshots on his mind.

Kaufmann's arrival was just one more reminder of how long it had been since Smith and his men had ventured onto Deck E, a full fourteen hours and counting. How much longer until they finished the quarantine and the stairwells could be reopened? Passengers could be misdirected for only so long.

"So nice to see you again," Ismay said. "However, I'm sorry to say that we'll be unable to reopen access to the lower decks tonight. I'd like to invite you . . ."

"I won't be plied with champagne any longer, Ismay," snapped Kaufmann. "I have no plans to leave the bridge until I'm allowed access to the lower decks. There's someone I need to see below, urgently. I'm through being cooped up."

The bridge telephone sounded. Mr. Humphries, a petty officer assigned to navigation and maps, answered the call. He listened briefly, then held out the receiver: "Mr. Wilde. It's the captain."

Ismay lunged for the phone, snatching it before Wilde could respond. "It's Ismay. Are we clear?"

Smith barked, "Close all watertight doors immediately. Every compartment down here must be barricaded shut."

Ismay's mouth opened in shock. When he noticed others watching, he shut it.

We're only a day's sail from reaching New York! he thought. *Won't closing the doors keep the firemen from fueling the boilers? Does Smith have any idea what he is proposing?* Ismay imagined men with wheelbarrows full of coal standing helplessly on the other side of metal doors as every boiler's fire died out. *Titanic* would fizzle to a halt in the middle of the sea. And there was Kaufmann, arms folded, waiting impatiently for him to hang up. God, how Ismay hated him. How this man—a competitor! A *German* competitor!—had even been allowed to purchase passage . . .

Smith growled into the phone. "Ismay, are you there? Do you hear me? We've died nearly a dozen deaths trying to get to this phone." When Ismay still didn't respond, Smith shouted, "Put Mr. Wilde on immediately."

Ismay said heartily with false good cheer, "That is *wonderful* news, Captain Smith. And with the engines running at full capacity, everyone aboard will be part of history when we set a new speed record."

"Full capacity?" asked Smith. "*Speed record?* Are you mad?" Smith was shouting to be heard over some grisly churning noise in the background that Ismay could not make out.

"Very well," said Ismay, smiling at the crew and the reviled Mr. Kaufmann. "We'll keep guards restricting access to the lower decks, if you insist."

"Shut those doors!" shouted Smith. "That is a direct order!"

"Already done," returned Ismay. "Every boiler is at full steam. We'll be in New York far ahead of schedule."

"Listen to me," said Smith gravely. "I don't know what you're doing, but every moment you waste, the more you damn this ship."

"I agree, of course, the best solution is to push on for New York. Thank you for all you've done, Captain. We're going to make it!" Ismay wheeled around hard to face the assembled crew members, feigning surprise when, in apparent excitement, he pulled the phone cord clean out of the receiver.

Ismay had made up his mind—*Titanic* would proceed at full steam. Smith was wrong. Whatever was happening below, the best chance for the rest of the passengers was to reach land as soon as possible. Ismay would pretend all was well and forestall a general panic as long as he could.

"The captain had an excellent report," Ismay announced, handing the detached receiver to a member of the crew. "He agreed with my strategy, Mr. Wilde, and wants you to continue at top speed. Let's do our jobs and not let him down."

"Aye," said a relieved Mr. Wilde. "I'll get someone working on that phone. All of you, back to your posts." The crew returned to their duties.

Ismay returned his attention to Mr. Kaufmann, who was still waiting with a hard look on his face. This time, Ismay did not conceal his annoyance. "Your place is not on the bridge, sir. It's time for you to leave."

"A fine performance," said Kaufmann, "but I know better."

Ismay hesitated. *Had the other side of his conversation been heard?*

"We're in the same game, Mr. Ismay. And sometimes what's necessary is to protect what you've so carefully crafted at all costs. I know a lie when I hear one."

J. Bruce Ismay's mind was racing. *How much does Kaufmann know? And how does he know it?* "What will it take to get you out of my sight, Kaufmann?" he asked bluntly.

"As before, there is an affair below that requires my immediate attention. You will see that I am allowed access. Either that or I will ensure that your first-class passengers, these influential members of worldwide high society, begin acting differently very soon. That won't be at all pleasant . . . as I'm sure you can imagine."

"I'll have your silence in exchange for passage below?" asked Ismay.

"You have my word."

"Very well," said Ismay, more than ready to give the bastard what he wished for.

33

Smith slammed the telephone to its resting spot. His anger circled the air like a thick-taloned eagle. No one in the bakery dared speak.

Even so, the room was hardly silent. The exhaust fan's motor grinded and groaned as the monsters continued to mindlessly launch themselves into the blades. On top of it all, in the distance a chorus of dogs barked in alarm—were ghouls attacking *Titanic*'s kennels as well?

"Captain," said Hargraves, finding the nerve to speak. "Was your order obeyed?"

"I was ignored," grunted Smith. "Ismay has the ship running at top speed, trying to set a *speed record!* We were cut off before I could say any more."

Shocked silence descended on the group.

Weiss was incredulous. "If the bridge doesn't close those doors, there won't be a single human left by the time we get to New York, no matter how fast!"

"Why does closing the doors matter at this point? Certainly after all we've seen on the way here, you don't consider that a real solution," said Hargraves. "If fleas are also carriers, then what hope is there? Fleas, rats, people—the disease could be everywhere by now."

"I am as shocked as you," said Weiss. "At every turn, this disease has defied my expectations."

"Still," said Andrews, "we don't know the extent of the spread for certain. If we can lower the watertight doors, we give *Titanic* a chance. If there are places the disease hasn't reached yet, they'll be protected by the doors. The plan isn't foolproof, but it's the best we have." Andrews looked at each of the group in turn; they were slumped exhausted against counters and cabinets. "In my estimation, it's all we have."

"That's all well and good," Hargraves remanded, "but the bridge has ignored us. Seems to me like the best course of action is to abandon ship."

"I will decide our next course of action," barked Captain Smith. "But we'll need our strength to carry out any plan. Drink. Find food and eat while I take some time to think."

The ragged group did as the captain ordered: gulped water from the sinks and ate prepared bread from trays that would never be delivered to the dining rooms. Weiss gnawed carefully, trying unsuccessfully not to reawaken the pain in his jaw. All the time, they stole glances at the exhaust fan, which still functioned but sounded more labored by the minute.

As Andrews chewed a roll, he fingered the telephone's connecting cord. "There might be a way to do it without the bridge," he said.

Captain Smith perked up. "What are you saying, Mr. Andrews?"

"If I can get to the watertight door just down the hall and inside the controller box, I might be able to rewire it and work all the watertight doors from here. I'm not sure. It's probably all or nothing. I'll either short the whole system and render it useless, or I might be able to slam every door."

"It's worth the gamble," decided Captain Smith.

"There are no guarantees," cautioned Andrews. "And I'll need tools."

"Be resourceful then, Mr. Andrews," said Captain Smith. "Let's do all we can to stop this thing."

Andrews got to work. First he cut and stripped the telephone wire with a bakery knife, and then he gathered metal cooking utensils that would serve as tools for prying into the box. Meanwhile, Captain Smith organized the others to carry out a plan, not only to reach the nearest watertight door but to destroy the zombie menace in the immediate area.

Filled with purpose, the group became reenergized. The watertight door was approximately thirty yards to the left down the corridor outside the bakery's front door. Across the corridor from the bakery was a kitchen. To the right, the kennels. Smith gave the marching orders: Andrews would head left to rewire the control box just beyond the watertight door. Smith and Hargraves would fight off any zombies who tried to stop him. Weiss and Louise would carry out Smith's plan in the kitchen.

Meanwhile, the shrieking moans emanating from the stewards' quarters seemed to be drawing every zombie on Deck F. An endless number continued to try to jam themselves into the exhaust fan. The sheer volume of flesh occasionally forced the rotating blades to stop. Any potential openings were filled with eviscerated body parts, so the eager creatures clawed away at the piles of dismembered torsos and limbs. Each time they cleared a path, the blades sped up again. The zombies were too uncoordinated and single-minded to solve this problem, and for now, the precarious blockade held. The motor groaned and smoked from the strain.

Captain Smith anticipated the moment the machinery ground to a complete halt. Preparations were complete, so he put his protective linen back over his head and instructed the others to do the same. He pocketed a small box of wooden matches he found above the stove. Then he drew Kabul and gave the signal for Hargraves to unlock and open the bakery door. A wandering zombie in a porkpie hat stumbled by at that moment, turning 'round in time to catch the glint off Smith's blade just before Kabul separated the creature's head from its neck.

The German and the girl made for the kitchen across from the bakery at top speed. They opened the burners on every oven, range, and stove, turning knobs as quickly as they could. Lou coughed as she released the gas, invisible but menacing. She managed a "thumbs up" at Weiss, and he grinned back at the girl.

At the same time, Andrews ran down the corridor and took the screws out of the watertight door's control box with the flat end of a butter knife. As he worked, Hargraves stood guard over him. Smith defended the bakery door, and it wasn't long before the fan motor finally seized and died. At the sound, Smith raised Kabul. As soon as zombies appeared in the doorway, he dispatched them one at a time. Yet the trickle swelled to a flood, and the captain was steadily forced backward. Hargraves started to leave his post by Andrews to help, but the captain ordered him back. He had just received aid from an unexpected source.

The dogs of *Titanic* barked furiously in their kennels, sent into fits of wild excitement by the dead scent of the zombies. The incessant baying distracted the zombies, who jerked and turned in the direction of the kennels. This gave Smith the openings he needed to detach the zombies' curiously tilted heads from their shoulders with methodical precision.

Andrews worked furiously at the watertight door, relieved that no undead attackers came from the fore of the ship. He tentatively prodded the exposed telephone wire into the electric lock. A cobalt-blue spark arced, indicating that he'd found the correct node. He snaked more copper wires inside the box, connecting them to the leads. Hargraves stood at the ready with his fire ax, prepared to do what he must should any fiends arrive from the other direction.

In the galley, Weiss pulled the linen closer to his mouth, coughing violently as the gas filled the room. Their job was done, and it was time to join the others. The German turned for Lou—but the girl was gone.

"No!" cried Weiss. He searched frantically beneath tables and behind moving carts. Had the beasts got her while Weiss's back was turned? "Louise! Lou?"

However, Lou was neither in the kitchen nor in the dead grasp of a zombie. She had snuck unseen past Captain Smith and to the kennels. She couldn't help it—she couldn't leave these animals to die. There was still something worth saving.

Dozens of dogs barked to beat the band—Pekinese and Pomeranians, spaniels and French bulldogs, terriers and Airedales. Their yelps grew louder at the sight of Lou. She crossly put a finger to her lips.

"You want the spooks to get you?" she asked in a hush, clicking open the cage doors and setting the animals free. "Now shut your yaps and run like the wind!"

Andrews finished connecting the wires. He then reached into his coat and brought out the last of his kerosene-filled squash balls. Some of the fuel had leaked through the pucker in the rubber ball, dampening his pocket, but there was still a satisfying heft of liquid inside. All was ready. "Let's go, let's go!" he pleaded. The corridor reeked of gas.

Smith dashed for the watertight door, joining Andrews and Hargraves. Not far behind was Weiss, who emerged distraught from the galley.

"Have you seen Lou?" he cried.

"She's supposed to be with you!" Captain Smith shouted.

From the far end of the corridor, more zombies lumbered into view, and a steady stream continued emerging from the now undefended bakery door.

Andrews wound two copper wires together and touched them to the inside of the metal box. A bright flash followed, but Andrews didn't even feel the charge singe all the way up his arm.

With a jerk and a clank, the watertight door began to descend, each chain link letting out a *clack* along the way. Andrews put an ear to the wall and listened. "I can hear the door in the deck above closing!" he shouted. "That did it! I think I got them all! " He looked around at the others, elated. "We've got twenty seconds till they finish closing."

"*Lou!*" Weiss shouted.

Then, as if unleashed by Apollo himself, a scrabbling pack of dogs scurried into the corridor. Some raced through the legs of angry zombies and away, while other dogs leaped to attack the diseased menace.

Weiss understood and yelled toward the kennels. "Louise, you must hurry! The doors are closing!"

Lou released the last dog, a tiny Airedale the size of a puppy. It seemed to sense the danger and latched onto its rescuer. The dog hovered at Lou's legs as if tied by an invisible leash. She gave it a few gentle kicks, but the pooch wouldn't run. "Fine, buster, have it your way," she said. She scooped the dog up in her arms and ran for the descending watertight door.

She stopped short: between her and the safety of the others stood half a dozen zombies. Weiss attacked the first creature he came to, a tall, slobbering monster in a black topcoat.

Lou bolted forward with the dog in the crook of her elbow like a stolen loaf of bread. Her only weapons were two talents the zombies lacked: agility and speed. She zigged and zagged between the monstrosities, darting below and beyond their swinging arms.

Weiss crippled another zombie's decaying leg by thrusting the knife stick through the side of the knee, trying to clear a path. Then the German fell and rolled underneath the lowering door. Lou sprinted for the opening, tiny dog yapping away in her ear.

"Get down!" shouted Andrews.

Lou slid—and then stopped with a jerk just before the door. The final zombie Weiss had toppled had grabbed Lou's collar as the girl went by. Even with a severed leg dangling by a tendon, the thick-necked zombie was strong as the man it had been in life. It slowly pulled the girl back.

"Help!" cried Lou.

Before any of the men could respond, the tiny dog leaped from her arms and sunk its teeth into the thick, undead fingers curled round the lacy neckline of Lou's best dress. The zombie howled at the small creature and clumsily tried to swat it away. But the terrier's determination was equal to the zombie's strength. With a low deep growl that seemed to come from an entirely different dog, the mutt tore off two of the zombie's fingers and broke its grip.

Two feet now separated the door from the floor. Weiss reached beneath the door and pulled Louise through with a furious tug.

"The dog!" cried Lou, scrambling forward and reaching back under the door. The terrier continued attacking the monster, which moaned furiously and swung the dog in an arc along the floor, but could not get rid of it.

Weiss snatched Lou away from the falling metal barrier, wrapping her in his arms so she could not escape again. Smith ignited the wick of the last squash ball and stepped back as Andrews swatted it using Kabul's broadside, sending the flaming ball through the narrowing gap beneath the watertight door.

Instantly, an explosion louder than thunder shook the air as the gas cloud ignited, and hellish flames belched out from beneath the heavy metal barrier just as it sealed tight to the ground with a heavy *thud*.

The ship's designer looked down and covered his mouth. A single severed hand lay there, flaming and missing two fingers.

34

"I wouldn't have believed it if I hadn't seen it with my own eyes," exclaimed Hargraves, stomping at the flaming hand triumphantly and pulling the linen from his face. "You did it with a butter knife no less!"

The men slapped Andrews on the back, laughing and shouting. They all removed their masks and whooped in celebration. Marvelous relief hung in the air like confetti.

"Well done," said Weiss. "Do you think the doors truly closed?"

"I can't say for certain, Mr. Weiss," answered Andrews. "But I think I closed them all!"

Captain Smith laid a weary hand on Andrews's shoulder. "That was some work, Thomas. I've seen men do much less with better tools at their disposal."

"What's wrong, Lou?" Weiss asked, seeing that Lou wasn't sharing their jubilation. "We did it!"

"That little mutt saved my life," the girl muttered. "Now she's gone like the rest of them." She sat against the wall and put her head against her knees, exhausted and cheerless.

The smiles faded on the men's faces. Captain Smith said, "The girl's right. Many are dead, and we should temper our joy. We are not out of the woods yet. First, we must reach the bridge and discover what has transpired elsewhere on *Titanic*."

"Certainly," said Hargraves, "the time has come to abandon ship."

Andrews blinked. "But there may still be hundreds of healthy people aboard *Titanic*, sir. We must gather the healthy and assess the damage. Surely, if we've contained the contagion, we won't abandon *Titanic* now?"

"Exactly, Mr. Andrews," Captain Smith said. "But that's a job for *Titanic*'s officers and crew. Mr. Hargraves, you've proved yourself more than a hero today. Continue with us to the top deck. If it comes time to abandon ship, we'll be sure you make it off safely."

The rush of their success and narrow escape was wearing off. "I have a pressing matter to attend to as well." Weiss eyed the men in turn. "You know by now it's not exaggeration to say that entire nations could be at risk if the infection escapes this ship. I must find the madman who stole that damned vial from me."

"Did I hear you right?" said Hargraves, eyes narrowing. "Are you saying *you* brought this disease aboard?"

Lou looked up from the floor.

Weiss stammered. He had forgotten not everyone present knew the story. "Yes, well, I was . . . searching for a cure. But the vial was stolen from me when—"

"How could you?" Lou sprung from the ground and lunged at Weiss. "My mum's dead because of you! Worse than dead! *You* brought this sickness onto *Titanic*!" She threw fists at the scientist's face and chest. Weiss didn't attempt to block the blows. Finally, Andrews grabbed the girl from behind and restrained her arms.

Something inside Weiss collapsed upon seeing the rage and pain in the girl's face. "It . . . it *is* my fault," he conceded. "To believe that I could be responsible for something so evil. I was a fool to think I could safeguard this Pandora's box . . ." He choked on his own words. "I'm surely doomed to hell for what I've done."

"Murderer," Lou whispered.

"That's enough," said Captain Smith gently, touching the girl's shoulder.

"He killed my mother!" Lou's red face screamed defiance.

"Louise," Smith said, "none of us can change what's done. We must leave judgment to God."

"All of this. The monsters, the dead. It's all your fault!" said Lou to Weiss. She shook free of Andrews, backed away from the men, straightened her skirt, and spat at Weiss.

"I deserve that," Weiss said, eyes on the floor. "I deserve your hatred."

"You deserve *worse*," shouted Lou. She turned and ran, sprinting up a set of stairs just down the corridor from the watertight door. Weiss started after her, but Captain Smith extended an arm to hold the German back.

"Let her mourn," counseled Smith. "Later you can make your peace with her, if she'll allow it." Captain Smith motioned with Kabul to the stairwell where Lou had just made her escape. "I believe you had no intention to set this scourge loose, but there's still a ledger to square. Begin by stopping this man from bringing it into the world."

Weiss bowed his head and nodded. "Up top is as good a place to start looking as any."

"I'll escort you, Mr. Weiss," said Hargraves, bouncing the fire ax in his hands. "Till we find him. Wherever you want to go."

"Good man, Hargraves," said the captain. "As for me, I need to remind Mr. Ismay who is in charge of *Titanic*."

"Let's hurry then," Andrews said. "I doubt the straightest path to the boat deck remains to us. It may take some minutes yet to reach the bridge."

Bruised and fatigued, the four men hobbled up the stairs together. Weiss was uncertain where he should begin searching, but the German agent was likely to be among the top decks, as far from the contagion as possible.

The floor suddenly lurched as they reached the first landing, sending the four men sprawling. The ship groaned from deep within, structural and ominous, accompanied by a long echoing screech. The stairwell railing vibrated violently with a low metallic hum as the men found their bearings.

"My God," said Hargraves. "What have the monsters done?"

Smith shook his head. "No zombie can rock a ship like that."

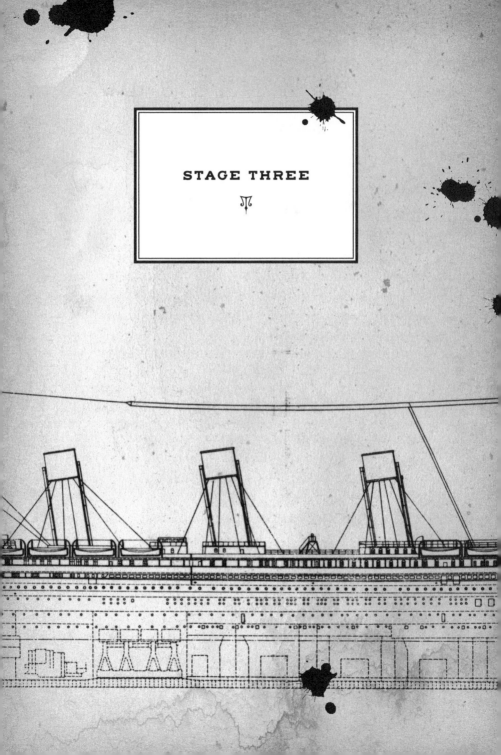

STAGE THREE

35

Ismay was enduring a brandy while a wealthy Indian doctor explained to him how he could cure aching joints, rheumatism, and a variety of other maladies with some sort of needle nonsense. Ismay hadn't heard a word, his mind preoccupied with preparations for docking in New York. Even arriving in the middle of the night, it was hard to see how he could avoid a press nightmare.

The jolt caught both men off guard, forcing them to catch their balance. The Indian didn't miss a beat, continuing to jabber on about the therapeutic effects of his stickpins. It was the chandeliers that worried Ismay with their sharp swing forward and the anxious tinkling of the glass. Ismay knew that rough waters would only cause a sway—and on his way to the lounge, the ocean's surface had been as smooth as a shaving mirror. Ismay mumbled an excuse and headed toward the wheelhouse.

Outside, he stopped in his tracks at the sound of scraping on the open promenade. A great mass of ice leaned against the rails. As the iceberg passed, bits sliced off and scattered across the deck. Just up the way, a few night-owl passengers picked up the shaved ice and made snowballs, playfully tossing them at one another. One of the gentlemen hollered to Ismay: "Say, is there any danger from this?"

"None!" returned Ismay through a clenched smile. "Just a bit of ice is all!"

Anyone could have followed Ismay's path to the wheelhouse: A deck chair kicked into the rails. The fragments of a clay water pitcher bashed off a table. A dented whiskey flask rifled off the bridge's steel exterior. He arrived to discover that First Officer William Murdoch had relieved Officer Wilde and was now at the command.

"For the love of God what's happening!" Ismay's eyes were wild, and his face was colored an unnatural shade. Murdoch had always been intimidated by J. Bruce Ismay; now the tycoon was absolutely frightening.

"We received an urgent notice from the crow's nest of ice straight ahead," replied Murdoch. "I gave the order 'Hard a'starboard,' but we still seem to have collided."

"I can bloody well see we've collided! What of the damage!?"

"We don't know yet, sir," admitted Murdoch. "The phone's just been repaired. Shall we alert the passengers that we've encountered an iceberg?"

"The passengers are enjoying winter sports on the promenade!" yelled Ismay. "I think they have an inkling we've hit ice! I want to know what you're going to do about it."

"Mr. Ismay," said Murdoch, trying to remain composed. "I'm going to have to ask you to please leave the bridge so we can right this ship."

"I'll leave when I'm damn well ready! Has there been more word from Smith?"

"Nothing as yet," said Murdoch. "Please remove yourself, sir. We've important work to do."

The crew stared at Ismay as if he were some sort of animal. "What are you lot gawking at?" he barked. "Full speed ahead!"

36

"Could that have been another vessel, Captain?" Andrews asked.

"I know what it feels like to collide with another ship. That was ice, sure as fate, and what lurks under the waterline is far more dangerous than what's seen floating above," replied Smith.

The four men got back to their feet in the stairwell. Captain Smith nodded to the architect. "Change in plans, Mr. Andrews. We must head below and assess the damage."

"*Titanic* is safe, Captain, that I can assure you," said Andrews definitively. He freely admitted ignorance and doubt about many things, but his faith in the ship's design was resolute. "Even if we've struck ice, as you say, it would have to be a more violent collision than the one we just felt. Besides, the watertight doors are already lowered. She'll make it to New York, I'll wager. You're better served up top where—"

"You and I are going below," the captain retorted.

"Yes, Captain," said Mr. Andrews. "Of course."

Smith turned to Weiss. "And you, Mr. Weiss, must delay your search. I need to enlist your services. Mr. Andrews, your notebook."

Andrews handed the captain his notebook and pen. Smith thumbed his way to an empty page, scribbled a command, and signed it.

Weiss's face collapsed. "Respectfully, Captain," said Weiss, "I believe my focus should be recovering the vial of the Toxic."

"By the time you find that needle, this haystack could be at the bottom of the ocean. Locate Mr. Murdoch on the bridge and deliver this order. I want lifeboats prepared as a precaution. He should expect to hear from me soon. Once this message is delivered, then you and Mr. Hargraves are free to search for your thief."

Weiss agreed reluctantly. "Yes, Captain."

"Very good," said Smith. "Mr. Andrews?"

Andrews nodded, summoning the will to plunge yet again into the unknown. "Below we go."

—————

Neither Weiss nor Hargraves spoke as they made their way up the stairs. Following Mr. Andrews's directions, they were to proceed to Deck Z, down a narrow hallway, then straight up a series of hatches directly to the bridge. Weiss was happy to have Hargraves along in case of more monsters, but even more to help with the thief. He could prove more dangerous than Weiss could handle alone.

As they ran, the adrenaline that had fueled Weiss through the previous twenty-four hours quickly gave way to fatigue and an overwhelming guilt. The child's accusations cut deep, and his wounded shoulder throbbed with each step. Weiss was sure he'd never been on his feet so long without rest, and his thigh muscles ached.

Weiss looked over to Mr. Hargraves, who appeared nearly as exhausted. His fine clothes were ripped and stained, and the gentleman's hair was wild. *I can only pray that none of us have been infected through a scratch, doomed like all these poor souls.* Then Weiss's thoughts ran to the first person he'd known to die from the plague—his sister, Sabine.

Six days after their twelfth birthdays, he fell ill with fever, chills, and muscle cramps. It was the bubonic plague. The doctors were never sure how he survived; they only said that some percentage always did. But Theodor was certain that he infected Sabine. She simply would not leave her brother alone and allow him to be sick all by himself.

The twins drew each other pictures from their sick beds—the two of them flying over mountains or taming lions—but the fun lasted only two days before they succumbed to painful swellings and dreadful aches. After more than a week passed, Theodor felt his strength begin to return, though he remained far from whole.

Theodor wasn't allowed to hold Sabine's hand. Instead, he stood outside her door and whispered encouragement, knowing that somehow she would hear. He could feel Sabine succumbing to the fever. He could hear her breathing, ragged and labored as the disease ravaged inside her. He filled his own lungs with air, trying to breathe for his twin.

As he felt her slip away, he promised to cure the sickness. Theodor imagined Sabine smiling at the sound of his words. There was nothing else he could do.

How would Sabine judge him now? He remained so far away from keeping his promise.

"According to Mr. Andrews, here's where we veer off for the bridge," said Hargraves.

"Yes, of course," Weiss said. "To the bridge."

Weiss and Hargraves made their way along the narrow Deck Z corridor that led to the hatches. They scanned their surroundings constantly, alert for sounds or signs of movement. Pipes painted bright white hung overhead, reflecting the light and making the hallway appear longer than the others. Weiss caught his breath and wiped his face with a ragged sleeve. *Pull yourself together,* he told himself. *There's still a chance.*

Weiss and Hargraves suddenly heard the pounding of feet running toward them. Not shuffling, but running. They stopped and prepared to meet whoever it was. Around a corner up ahead a man emerged. It was Emil Kaufmann. He was carrying a gun.

Kaufmann stopped running and smiled—a tight, smug grin—then approached confidently. "You're a hard man to track down, Herr Weiss," said Kaufmann. He raised his gun and trained it on Weiss's forehead. "But surely you knew there was no real chance of escape to America. It's time to end this. The Kaiser would like the Toxic back, if you please."

Weiss stared blankly at Kaufmann. "I . . . I don't have the Toxic, of course. You took it from me."

Hargraves set down his ax and reached inside his coat.

He must have one of the captain's guns, Weiss thought desperately. *The odds are even.*

But Hargraves did not withdraw a gun. He produced a stainless-steel cylinder, ten inches long, and slightly bigger than the glass vial it contained. "I have the Toxic," he said in fluent German.

"*You?* You have the Toxic?" asked Weiss in shock.

"Ah, so it's you," said Kaufmann. "Excellent. This will be even easier." Kaufman chuckled. "From the looks of you, I can see why you've had difficulty reporting to Herr Moltke."

Hargraves slipped the cylinder back into his jacket, joining the laughter. "I've had an eventful voyage." Then he swiped the knife-stick from a stunned Weiss and threw it behind them, back into the stairwell.

"Please, both of you, listen to reason," pleaded Weiss. "Don't take the vial back to Germany! Mr. Hargraves or whoever you are, you've seen its horrors firsthand!"

The Agent ignored Weiss and addressed Kaufmann. "May I have the honor of silencing this traitor with your pistol?"

Kaufmann considered the request, then handed his revolver to the Agent with a nod. "Certainly. You've earned the right. Let justice be served."

The Agent took the gun and promptly shot Kaufmann in the chest. Kaufmann's eyes went wide and his mouth opened to speak, but only a gurgling sound emerged as he slumped to the floor.

"But . . ." Words failed Weiss. Nothing made sense.

"Herr Moltke has different ideas than I about how to use your discovery. I have certain needs that must come before Germany's. We are both traitors in our own way, Herr Weiss. We are both interested in doing what is . . . right."

Weiss still didn't understand, but he knew the Kaiser's man meant him ill. Weiss glanced down the corridor to the hatch that led, eventually, to the bridge. He could make a break for it, but he would be gunned down inside of ten steps.

"I need to conserve my ammunition, Herr Weiss," said the Agent, sliding the revolver inside his jacket. As his hand emerged, it held a familiar tool, the corridor lights glinting off its needle-nosed tip.

"Since you have fought bravely beside me, I will try to make this quick."

37

"Oh my," said Andrews.

The squash court was deserted. Smith and Andrews stood alone on the observation level where they could peer down into the mail room below on Deck G. Water was flooding in, perhaps a foot deep already. Letters and assorted small packages were floating on the floor as men tried to scoop them up.

"Aye, it's worse than I feared. We need to get a better look. Let's head for the fireman's tunnel below." Captain Smith broke for the stairwell, but Andrews didn't immediately follow. The ramifications of what he was seeing weakened his legs, which would not move.

Titanic was the crowning achievement of Andrews's life. He drove himself for years to make it the finest ship in the world. He had often envisioned her steaming majestically into the safe harbor of New York, and he'd gone so far as to select a painting for the first-class smoking room depicting such a scene.

Though it felt a lifetime ago, it had been only a handful of hours since he had stood on nearly the same spot and noticed the loose joint on a corner piece of window trim. He'd recorded it in his notebook. Looking down at the rising water covering the squash court, Andrews felt the pad of paper in his pocket. He wondered if his attention to detail had been reduced to irrelevancy. Then he ran after Captain Smith to find out.

The seawater was so cold the firemen's hands were blue. Undaunted, crewmen rushed back and forth, valiantly trying to string together enough hose to pump out the areas taking on water. One of them, a young fellow with a full head of copper-red hair, saw the captain and ran over to give him the report.

"How bad is it, lad?" Smith asked.

"We're in a tight pickle, sir. Numerous compartments are flooding." The young man wiped a stream of dark blood from his nose and onto his pants. Smith and Andrews exchanged a dark glance.

"How many?" asked Andrews.

"Six is the last number I heard."

Smith looked to Andrews, but hope had drained from the designer's face. He gave the smallest, most imperceptible shake of his head. The captain nodded his understanding. He gave the seaman a reassuring smile and said loudly, "You men are doing your captain proud."

"Thank you, sir. To top it all, there's this bad flu going around." The sailor launched into a string of uncomfortable hard coughs, doubling over.

"How many are ill?" asked Smith once the man recovered.

"Pretty much all of us, sir. Some worse than others, but to a man everybody's puny with it. To be honest, some more than puny."

Smith lifted his chin. "Carry on. Mr. Andrews and I need to finish our inspection."

When the sailor was out of earshot, Andrews confessed, "She'll float with four compartments flooded but no more than that." Tears welled up in his eyes. "This ship will sink, sir."

"How long do we have?" the captain asked.

"An hour, perhaps an hour and a half, no more."

"Even with the pumps?"

"Those will only buy minutes. They're rated to handle two thousand tons of water an hour. From what I've seen, that amount is flooding in every five minutes. And not to put too fine a point on it, sir, but *the men*. Everyone down here is doomed." The tears finally broke through.

For a moment, Captain Smith felt angry. What had Ismay been thinking, running *Titanic* full bore? At that speed, *Titanic* had no chance to evade an iceberg. Smith's anger waned as he watched his crew, working valiantly but in vain to contain the flooding. In their condition, *Titanic* would have been doomed, no matter her speed. At least drowning would spare them from the infection's horror.

Smith put his hand on Andrews's shoulder. "It's a tragedy, Thomas," the captain said. "We have to save who we can. Agreed?"

Andrews wiped the tears from his eyes and collected himself. "That, sir, is why you are captain of *Titanic*. All that matters is to save as many as possible. I'll follow you to the bottom of the Atlantic."

"Then let's go. We must get the healthy passengers off this ship—while ensuring that the infected stay aboard. If *Titanic* is going down, we'll make sure this scourge sinks with it."

The captain led the way to the stairwell, but once again, Thomas Andrews hesitated. Surveying the havoc a final time, he pulled the small notepad from his pocket and pitched it into the knee-deep water, leaving the details for the devil.

30

The Agent sprang with his pliers, bearing down at the base of Weiss's throat.

Desperately, Weiss grabbed the Agent's wrist with both hands, stopping the weapon. Without hesitation, the Agent violently slammed his forehead into Weiss's nose with a sickening *crack*. As if observing the scene from above, Weiss thought, *"seeing stars" isn't just a figure of speech.*

"Why?" Weiss managed to grunt. "Why were you helping us below?"

"Quite the contrary," said the Agent, his breath cool and stale against Weiss's skin. "You helped me. After confirming you lied about the cyanide, and finding you gone from the linen closet, I thought simply to hide till we reached America. But the infection was more powerful than I imagined. I was surrounded by the sick and running for my life when we met. Joining your band was my best chance."

The Agent pressed harder with his tool, relentlessly, and Weiss gasped as the cold steel met his throat. Weiss grunted, "Don't leave this ship with the vial. Mothers have been transformed into monsters, for God's sake. No one deserves such a fate."

The Agent's eyes twitched madly as the ship's bow began to dip into the Atlantic. "Some people most certainly do, Herr Weiss. Some people do. And it will be even more horrific than I dared dream, thanks to you. Imagine the havoc, the power in just a single drop. That's all it will take to—"

"You took everything from me!" screamed Lou, as she dropped from the hatch at the end of the hallway. The Agent wheeled around, and as he did, a bright white flash burst from Lou's outstretched hands. The flare gun's recoil sent the girl reeling backward into the wall as the burning projectile struck the Agent hard in the middle of his chest. The shell bounced to the ground and exploded, blinding Weiss as he rolled away.

The Agent slapped wildly at his burning hair and jacket. He careened into the wall and stumbled recklessly down the hallway. Lou braced herself, reloaded, and fired again. The flare hit the Agent square in the back, knocking him down. He rolled on the floor to douse the flames, then got up and disappeared into the stairwell.

Weiss was trying to blink the sight back to his eyes. "Louise!" he called out. She ran up to him, and he smiled as his hands found her shoulders.

"It's Lou," she said.

"Lou," said Weiss. He could see her smiling at him. "Are you hurt?"

Lou shook her head. Weiss asked anxiously, "Where did Mr. Hargraves run off to?"

"I didn't see. Too much smoke. But he's gone now."

Weiss scooped the girl off her feet, exhilarated despite himself. "Where did *you* run off to?"

"Doesn't matter anymore," Lou responded. "I heard what Mr. Hargraves said and . . ." She dropped her eyes, a guilty look coming over her face, then threw her arms around him tight. "Now I know what's what."

Weiss suddenly understood and returned the embrace. The flare was originally meant for him. "Lou. I'd give my own life if I could bring your mother back. I'm sorry."

"I know," she whispered. "But we have to stop Mr. Hargraves."

"You must get off this boat," said Weiss. "Leave Hargraves to me."

"You can't do it alone," said the girl. "I'm helping you, and I'd like to see you try and stop me." She balled her fists.

Weiss laughed despite himself, bending over to pick up flare balls that were rolling very slowly toward the bow of the ship. "Let's get going, Lou. I don't know how much longer *Titanic* has."

Weiss and Lou took off at a run and up the narrow stairwell the Agent had taken. They stopped short at a jog in the stairs. Ahead, a makeshift gate had been forcibly moved aside and a young officer lay motionless on the steps, his head twisted at an awkward angle.

"Crikey, the monsters must have fought their way up," said Lou.

"I don't think so," said Weiss. He approached the dead man warily. The officer's eyes remained open with a terrified expression. But except for his ruptured neck and the pool of blood draining from it, he was otherwise uninjured: nothing had feasted on him, nor did he show any signs of infection. The dead man hadn't been ravaged by a zombie. Weiss knew a different kind of monster had caused the wound.

39

Kabul clanked against the captain's side as he and Andrews raced up step after step, past Deck G, past Deck F, on their way to the bridge. The sound of a woman screaming echoed in the stairwell. The captain cursed loudly and picked up his pace. Andrews followed as closely as he could. Even at sixty-one years of age, Captain Smith wasn't easy to keep up with.

Finally, they found the source of the screams: Two small children and their mother cowered on a landing, chased into the corner by a hulking zombie. From half a flight down, Smith called out. "Hey, you big ugly lout! Over here!"

The creature grunted at the sound of the captain's voice and turned. It was Joe Clench, or what was left of him, and he made the most imposing and horrifying zombie Smith and Andrews had seen yet.

Clench roared at the two men and took an awkward step toward them, away from the mother and her children. Not a brow raised in recognition on the behemoth's face. With plodding steps it descended three stairs. Blackish ooze ran from the corner of the monster's mouth. The repugnant effluence dribbled down to stain his uniform. The man was gone, but the rotted body lived.

"Run up those stairs as fast as you can," shouted Smith to the mother. "Get up top and board a lifeboat. We're abandoning ship." Without a word, the family ran.

The captain felt a pang of guilt—by sending Clench and the other men off for welding torches, he'd sentenced them to a horrible fate. "I won't let you suffer any further, Clench," said Smith, "even if you were a pain in the arse." The captain tried to draw Kabul, but it didn't come out cleanly, stopping in the sheath. That was all the time the zombie needed to reach the small landing.

"Run, Captain," hollered Andrews.

"Never!" growled Smith. Finally, the blade slipped free. A skillful feint to the zombie's midsection drew its arms down, then Smith swung mightily at Clench's defenseless neck and buried the blade several inches deep.

But Kabul was no longer up to the task. Weakened earlier by holding back the bakery fan, the blade snapped at the nicked point that caused it to stick in the sheath. Most of Kabul remained lodged in the beast's vertebrae. Smith was left with little more than the hilt and a pitiful stub of metal in his hand.

The zombie didn't even react to the sword stuck in its gashed neck. As in life, Joe Clench wasn't one to let a flesh wound stop a fight. One arm swiped viciously, sending the captain sprawling to the ground. Kabul's hilt spun away, and the zombie fell on top of Smith, enveloping him in its massive arms. Its clawing and gnashing about the captain's head was shocking and relentless.

"Hey, Mr. Clench!" yelled Andrews, from two steps below.

The zombie turned at the sound of a living voice. As it did, Andrews leapt and punched with all his might, using the rounded portion of Kabul's pommel, and struck the zombie dead in the mouth, knocking out its remaining teeth. Andrews kept pummeling its face until Mr. Clench fell away.

Andrews tried to help Smith to safety, but the captain would have none of it. He charged the zombie as it rose, despite the fact that it could no longer see. The force of Andrews's blows had knocked out the ghoul's eyes, which now dangled grotesquely from their sockets.

Smith wrenched what was left of Kabul from the zombie's neck and rammed the broken blade into its ear, all the way up to the knuckles. Clench fell to the ground like a tree. Exhausted, the captain regarded yet another of his former crew members he'd been forced to kill. "Goodbye, Mr. Clench, I'm sorry." Then he slumped to the floor himself.

As Andrews approached, Smith said firmly, "Don't touch me."

Then he looked up, and Andrews was stunned at the many deep gashes and black-colored cuts atop the captain's head. The captain sagged against the landing wall, his head hung low.

"I am going down with the ship, Andrews," Captain Smith said. "You are to report to the bridge and convey my order to launch all lifeboats."

"The men need you, sir," protested Andrews. "What if the chaos down here also reigns above? You can will yourself to remain in control."

"My will," scoffed Smith, "is to not endanger anyone aboard this ship. I can't be trusted with command any longer."

"You still possess all your faculties, Captain," Andrews pleaded. "Perhaps you don't have a lot of time, but neither does *Titanic*. This ship needs its leader." He picked Smith's cap off the ground. "There are innocent people to save. Be a beacon to them, sir."

Andrews handed Smith his cap. "This will cover most of the wounds to your scalp. And as the hours pass, if your condition worsens . . ." Andrews sighed. "The sea awaits."

Captain Edward Smith donned the cap, stood up, and nodded. "You're quite right, Thomas. I will fulfill my duties, 'til the end."

Smith reached out to shake Andrews's hand, then realizing that was no longer prudent, saluted him instead.

40

MARCONI ROOM.

MONDAY, APRIL 15, 1912. 12:29 A.M.

Radio operator Harold Bride returned from a trip to the wheelhouse, where he had breathlessly reported the news to First Officer Murdoch that a ship, *Carpathia,* was coming as fast as she could. "Less than four hours away and putting all her steam into it!" The news seemed to brighten the dark mood on the bridge. Bride was determined to find more help.

"Always seems to be a dozen ships around until you really need one," groused Jack Phillips, tapping away on his wireless with tobacco-stained fingertips. The senior Marconi man knew the ship was compromised, but his faith in the indomitable *Titanic* was steadfast. After all, other ruptured ships had stayed afloat for days. Still, the peculiar guttural rasp from below made listening for incoming messages more difficult than usual. "I've been sending *CQD! CQD!* for an hour. Maybe we'd have better response if I said we were overcome by pirates."

CQD was one of the first codes Bride had learned, a distress signal developed for the world's new wireless system. *CQ,* Bride knew, basically meant "stop sending all those damn messages and pay attention!" while the *D,* of course, was for "distress."

Bride had an idea. "Try the new one, why don't you? 'Save Our Souls' might scare up something."

"Anything for a change of pace," agreed Phillips. He started tapping and employed the latest international distress signal for the first time:

S-O-S. S-O-S. S-O-S.

41

BOAT DECK.

MONDAY, APRIL 15, 1912. 12:57 A.M.

Many concerned faces confronted Captain Smith and Andrews as they emerged on the boat deck. Yet to their great relief, they saw that the zombie menace had not yet arrived topside.

Crew members were trying to organize the rattled passengers, many still in their nightclothes, and announcing that the imminent evacuation was strictly for precautionary measures. Meanwhile, desperate signal flares screamed across the night sky, casting otherworldly light over the crowds on the boat deck. Anxiety had not yet become panic, but anyone with a head for arithmetic could see there would not be enough lifeboats for all.

"Andrews," Captain Smith said, "we need to find Weiss straight away."

Andrews ran to a nearby cargo crane and climbed up the ladder into darkness, giving him a better vantage point. He surveyed the deck, his head swiveling from right to left until he spotted his target. "I have them," Andrews shouted down. He pointed to where Lou and Weiss were standing on a bench and scanning the crowd themselves. The captain hurried over to them.

"We're trying to find Mr. Hargraves," exclaimed Lou. "He tried to kill Mr. Weiss! He's the one who stole . . ."

"The vial with the Toxic," finished Weiss. "Hargraves is the Kaiser's agent, he had it all along." Weiss gritted his teeth. "I'm not going to let him off this ship. He . . ."

Smith cut him off. "I'm ordering you to make sure no one is allowed on the lifeboats that exhibits any signs of the sickness. It can't leave this ship . . . in any form."

"But—" Weiss began.

"There is no other way off this ship than those lifeboats. You'll have no better opportunity to find your man and what he stole. I shall persevere to keep order and ensure the safety of those who are allowed to depart."

Weiss agreed with the plan. It was more practical than any kind of search he could undertake on his own. Rather than seeking out the Kaiser's man, Weiss would wait for the Agent to show himself.

Lou then asked, "Where's your sword, sir?"

"Broken. Its time had come," Smith replied. "Now go and do as I've said."

"Yes, sir," Lou barked.

Weiss searched the captain's face, and what the German found made it difficult to say "Yes, sir," and obey the order. But he did.

First Officer Murdoch had taken charge of seamen working feverishly to lower the odd-numbered lifeboats on *Titanic*'s starboard side, while Chief Officer Wilde supervised men lowering the even-numbered boats on the port side.

No good spot existed for Weiss to set up a mass inspection, so he did his best: he formed a line on the engineer's promenade, port side. His job was to send passengers through to the waiting lifeboats, once they were determined clear of infection. Because the passengers' numbers were so great, Weiss enlisted several junior officers to assist him. He gave them a rough outline of the situation: a serious infection was present on the ship. They needed to detain anyone who was feverish, complained of headaches, or most serious of all, had any dark fluid coming from their nose, mouth, or ears. Weiss refrained from explaining what happened next. Finally, he instructed the officers to be on the lookout for a man with slicked-back hair and a pencil-thin mustache. The man was a murderer who should be arrested.

Walking up and down the passenger line, Wilde and Murdoch made it known that no one would leave *Titanic* without verification that they were fit for rescue. The passengers, nearly all first- and second-class, submitted to the inspections—for all they knew, it was normal protocol to answer questions about their general health and to have eyes, ears, and mouth inspected by a medical man before abandoning ship.

As the inspections got underway, Lou stood by Weiss, acting as a second set of eyes to search for Hargraves and the Toxic. They'd seen no sign yet of the man Lou had nearly incinerated just an hour before.

The ship's store of handguns was lost below to the zombie menace. To keep order in any scenario, Chief Officer Charles Lightoller rounded up all weapons he could find for crowd control. Fifth Officer Harold Lowe, a stocky sailor with squinty eyes, revealed a pair of Browning semi-automatics that he'd smuggled aboard. "Thought they might come in handy if I ever ran into trouble," he admitted sheepishly.

"Trouble it is," said Lightoller, ignoring the rule violation. "But no shooting. Wave them around and holler a bit if anyone tries to get wise."

Two Catholic priests wandered among the waiting passengers, offering comfort. Six older men in topcoats gathered around the first stack, smoking pipes and trying to look the part of elders. Lou watched as a tearful father still in his nightclothes bid farewell to his two young sons, touching their chins and transferring responsibility for their mother onto their slight shoulders.

Eventually, a small mob of angry men formed in the inspection line. The largest hollered that they ought not wait any longer. His fellows agreed; they broke out of line and rushed Lifeboat 2, intent on commandeering the craft. Lightoller jumped in after them, brandishing one of the Brownings and threatening to do in any man who didn't abdicate in favor of women and children. The ploy worked, even though Lightoller's gun wasn't loaded.

Weiss was surprised that nearly all of the passengers looked healthy. Perhaps closing the watertight doors had done some good after all. So far, he'd found only two cases of infection, a pair of young, black-haired brothers. Swallowing hard, Weiss had sent them to be quarantined in the officers' cabins by able seamen. Both children were in the early stages of the illness, with just traces of ooze in their saliva, but each was infected just the same. "We're going to put you on a better boat very soon," he told them, offering kindness over honesty. "Invent some games to play while you wait."

The continued absence of the Agent was making Weiss anxious, and he considered other possibilities: perhaps the Kaiser's man had commandeered one of the lifeboats and escaped before *Titanic*'s crew started the evacuation. But surely news of a missing lifeboat would have reached Weiss by now. Maybe the man had his own means of escape—a military craft, perhaps an inflatable. But then what? Such a thing couldn't traverse the ocean. It would need a ship or submarine rendezvous. While Weiss couldn't dismiss the notion entirely, it seemed unlikely. *The simplest explanation is probably correct,* thought Weiss. *He's still on board, and I'm going to find him.*

Lifeboats had been steadily filled and lowered without incident. Yet a sense of panic was escalating as *Titanic*'s deck tilted farther toward the water. No rescue ships were appearing on the dark horizon. On one lifeboat, a woman screamed for her husband. Fewer than a dozen lifeboats remained to be loaded, and Weiss would make sure one young lady got aboard. He took Lou by the arm.

"We ain't found him yet!" cried Lou, realizing what was happening. "And I ain't leaving until we get 'im!"

"It's for your own good, Lou," Weiss replied, motioning for a nearby able seaman. "Mr. Buley, hold her while I conduct my inspection."

"Get your mitts off me. You know I got no sickness," Lou growled, pulling her arms from Buley's grasp. "No spook ever got his teeth into me and you're the witness, so you can keep your doctor visit."

Weiss spoke quietly, so others wouldn't hear, as he started his exam: "You've seen how many have already died on this ship, Lou. More are about to die. Do you know how many of those men standing over there would trade places with you? They're losing everything. Don't be a fool."

"I already lost everything," said Lou. "Let me help you get Hargraves! He tried to kill me, too, you know!"

"I'm not giving you a choice," said Weiss, finishing his check, satisfied. He motioned to the able seaman. "Mr. Buley, please escort this young lady to Lifeboat 6."

"Wait!" cried Lou, pulling away from Buley. "You want me on a lifeboat? Then you come with me."

Weiss blinked. "You want me to . . . ?"

"You could find your cure in Iowa, even without that vial. I know you could," Lou pleaded, touching the tattered cuff of Weiss's shirt. "I'll be your assistant. I'm going to be a scientist, you know. And you could stay with us. I'm sure Uncle George would let you . . ."

"Lou, I can't leave until I retrieve what I came here with," said Weiss. "You know that I have to stay."

Lou blinked the wet from her eyes.

"Go to Iowa, become a scientist," Weiss said. "Just the way your mother would have wanted."

Weiss stuck out a hand for Lou to shake and seal their deal. Lou threw herself into Weiss's arms and hung on tight. The warmth of the girl's face burned into Weiss's neck, and he was overcome with emotion from everything that had happened: his escape from Germany, his capture and the loss of the vial, the battle with the zombies belowdecks, the futility of trying to control the disease. Weiss wept, and he thanked God for Lou's forgiveness.

"Lots of people waiting," Lou said finally, pulling away. "I'll do you proud in America."

42

The zombies were contained no longer.

The able seamen guarding the stairwells above Deck Z were no match for the undead. One by one, the sailors were overrun by sheer numbers. Atop one stairwell, a soft-hearted seaman opened his Bostwick gate to let a frantic, seemingly healthy family by, but he didn't close it fast enough to stop a rush of pursuing monsters, destroying the gate and the guard himself.

If anything, the evacuation had worsened the situation. The *Titanic* crew's announcements and the ensuing shouts of the worried passengers only served to alert the zombies on the decks below to the presence of healthy flesh.

On Deck B, dozens of ghouls steadily emerged from multiple stairwells in ravenous desperation. Lurching through an empty restaurant toward the cabins of *Titanic*'s wealthiest first-class passengers, the zombies upended upholstered chairs and stumbled toward the sounds ahead. Screams were quickly silenced and replaced with cruel, guttural moans, which echoed off the oak panels.

Many of the luxury cabins were empty, their occupants having long since escaped to the top deck, some already safely away on lifeboats. But a fair number had stayed behind to dress properly, mortified at the possibility of being seen in their nightclothes. They paid for their vanity.

The dead descended on the living in their opulent staterooms. Former passengers from steerage feasted on the delicate-boned faces of ladies with hair piled high under feathered hats and pulled at limbs inside elegant French couture. Bankers with silver sideburns were yanked down from behind. Skulls were gnashed, and stylish topcoats were ripped apart.

Mr. Henry Hollister, a retired barrister, shouted, "Burn in hell, demon!" before firing his silver revolver four times into a young undead man's head and chest. Unfortunately, the sound of Hollister's weapon and voice attracted three more creatures, and he was out of ammunition.

Titanic's luxury cabins reverberated with sounds befitting a slaughterhouse, and glossy white walls were stained crimson. The frenzy lasted less than half an hour and left the entire deck decimated. The staircases beckoned with the sound of more prey above.

"Be British, boys, be British," Smith commanded to a group of men on the open deck who were desperately trying to bribe an officer in exchange for secure passage on a lifeboat. "It's women and children first." The shamed men relented, deferring to the captain's authority.

"It's as I predicted, sir," Andrews noted. "You are needed."

Smith nodded. The passengers were frightened and rightfully so. Even on a sinking ship, the sight of Captain Edward Smith—his unruffled figure a pillar of composure in the face of calamity—held off the threat of complete pandemonium. Now if Smith could only bring some order to the chaos surging inside his own body.

Smith had progressed much more quickly into Stage Two of the infection than he would have expected. He wondered if he had become infected long before his battle with Clench, though perhaps the location and severity of Clench's bites had hastened the Toxic's path to his brain. He had never experienced this kind of discomfort—and over a lifetime of soldiering and seafaring, he'd been burnt, stabbed, and beaten. He felt like the hull of an old steel ship, rusting from the inside. There was a dull, pervasive itch throughout his internals, more irritating than painful. He was mostly able to ignore it.

What couldn't be brushed aside was the inescapable ringing inside his head, a high whine that emanated directly from the middle of his skull. The clamor increased in pitch and intensity with each passing minute. As it grew, he could feel it overwhelm his concentration, even his intellect, effectively drowning out all higher functions. The shrill screeching was making him agitated in darkly violent ways, inciting base passions that rattled his windows into reason. When those shattered, he would no longer be human.

A lifeboat was preparing to launch and still loading passengers. "Go, Andrews," Smith commanded. "It's time. You've served with honor. Now save yourself."

Andrews thought to protest, but did not argue upon seeing the look in the captain's eyes. "Thank you, sir. We did the best anyone could. I'm off to see safe harbor."

After Andrews departed, Captain Edward Smith turned and let go a moan of agony, his shallow, rotten breath visible in the frigid air of the forward deck. Amid the commotion of the lifeboats, no one heard his throaty groan. It was a good thing, too. He was just cognizant enough to realize passengers were still watching him closely for signs of panic. As long as he remained calm, so would they.

Ahead, Weiss and *Titanic*'s crew continued loading women and children into the few lifeboats remaining on the bow, even as that part of the ship dipped dangerously near the water's surface. There was nothing more he could do. Smith summoned what sanity remained and strode toward the aft portion of the ship. He would stop by Mr. King's old cabin and procure a solid pair of handcuffs.

The sounds of terror rang in the night sky.

Captain Smith saw that total anarchy reigned on the promenade at the ship's rear. Zombies were emerging onto the boat deck from stairwells leading up from the first-class passenger cabins. Nearly everyone, even a few crew members, fled in terror from these living horrors, though most were trying in vain to hold them back. Sadly, Smith watched several men attempt to batter and wrestle the creatures to the ground, only to be overcome; the uninitiated did not know how to fight such an unrelenting foe. Except for the few ghouls stopping to feast on the heads and bodies of the fallen, the zombies' slow yet deliberate charge raged mostly unchecked.

Uninfected passengers were quickly realizing that running for the bow was their only chance. An elderly couple understood they were too slow to escape, choosing to hold each other in their final moment before being ravaged by five devils. The increasing tilt of the deck caused many to slip and fall, zombie and person alike. One gentleman with a rusty goatee attempted a leap over a fallen zombie but slid all the way down the deck and under the rails, tumbling into the icy waters below.

Captain Smith could see that the fleeing passengers were inadvertently leading the murderous mass toward *Titanic*'s stem, where the final evacuations were proceeding. If the zombies reached the lifeboats before they were away, the catastrophe would be total and complete. Smith needed more men to have any chance of delaying the pack long enough.

Smith spied Ismay fleeing for a collapsible that was being unfurled on the officers' deck. To his credit, the head of the White Star line had helped load passengers earlier, but now he was running for his life. The captain intercepted him, swallowing a mouthful of fluid dark enough to write with. "Mr. Ismay," he called, "join the fight. We need every man."

Ismay saw the black dribbling through Smith's beard. He caught his breath. "Dear God, not you, too."

"We must stop them before they reach the lifeboats," said Smith.

"Don't come near me," Ismay shouted, terror in his eyes as he backed toward the collapsible.

"Bruce, don't," implored Smith. "There are still lives to save." The captain could barely hear himself talk above what sounded like the mating call of one million cicadas echoing inside his skull, and for the first time he felt the urge to attack.

An inhuman sound escaped his mouth, voicing a combination of rage and something like hunger—but not to fill his stomach, not exactly. He staggered forward before the look of fear on Ismay's face brought the captain back to humanity. Ismay stumbled backward into the collapsible and pulled the strings of a life vest tight. "Launch this thing now!" he screamed, and the crew pushed the lifeboat free of the side.

Smith halted, again tamping down his unholy compulsion, and called out one last time in a strangled voice: "If you leave on that boat, you'll regret it forever. Live as a coward or die a hero!"

Ismay did not reply as the lifeboat lowered out of sight. Smith turned to see the advancing mob of zombies loping inexorably toward him, one gruesome woman literally dragging a leg. The tilt of the slick deck was causing them to lean almost to the point of tipping over. Their dead stares fixed on the uninfected passengers crowded around the final lifeboats just ahead.

Smith's decaying mind lost its tether to the present amid a jumble of memories. For a moment, he returned to the embassy in Kabul, as he prepared to rush forth and visit his rage on the enemy closing in. "It's our final stand, boys!" Smith cried. "Will no one join me?"

A firm hand grasped Captain Smith's shoulder. Smith spun hard, but did not recognize the young face. He was forced to read the lad's lips: "How may we help, Captain? We are at your service."

43

A plume of dark smoke spilling from the steamer's stacks did little to interrupt the serene backdrop of lazy clouds mingling with friendly blue sky. The ship, having completed its journey, cleaved into Plymouth Harbor, leaving in its wake a collection of sailboats whose masts were graced with the orange hue of a beautiful sunrise.

Just ahead to the port side, two fishermen sat in a small rowboat. The one in the bow was trying to get in a final cast before the huge vessel churned up the calm water and ran off the fish. Soon the ship would pass them. Soon it would finally be home.

The painting Thomas Andrews had purchased for *Titanic* hung above the fireplace in the first-class smoking room. It was entitled *Safe Harbor*. Andrews calmly pulled up a chair. He was at peace, smiling at the last thing he would ever see.

44

Weiss heard the moans of the emerging zombies, and he hastened his inspections. All the while, he searched the crowds for the German agent. The man was still on the damned boat; Weiss knew it in his bones. The few lifeboats that remained were filling fast.

Weiss ignored the outer trappings of face after face and focused on spotting those sharp, intense brown eyes. He'd recognize them no matter the disguise. Then a commotion drew his attention. One of the ship's quartermasters struggled with the next passenger in line.

"I am not ready to leave this ship!" shouted a small woman wrapped in expensive furs and oversized, extravagant jewelry. She clawed at the quartermaster, who looked ready to throw her overboard on general principle.

"Hold her arms tight," instructed Weiss as he thumbed the well-powdered flesh below her eyes, forcing them open so he could clear the *grande dame* for rescue. She thrashed her head this way and that as Weiss tried to examine her nostrils, ears, and gums.

"The indignity!" she screamed.

"Madame, I assure you, this is absolutely necess—"

"I'm not talking about your bloody health inspection!" squawked the woman. "This brute forcibly removed me from my cabin before I could find my good hair! Wait until Mr. Ismay hears how you treated me!"

Weiss paused, remembering. This was the same woman Lou had pointed out during boarding, the distinguished older lady with the absurd silver-blue hair. "Your *good* hair?" asked Weiss.

"Stolen!" cried Lady Cardeza. "Miss Anna placed it on the wig stand when I went to sleep. Hair doesn't just stand up on its hind legs and go for a stroll. Where is the captain? I demand an investigation!"

"Put her on a boat," said Weiss, standing now to survey the remaining passengers. With the sound of the wailing Lady Cardeza fading to the port side, Weiss strained in the dim light to spot the woman's wig. He cursed silently. Once again, the German agent was one step ahead of him. Weiss had alerted *Titanic*'s officers to watch for a man fleeing the ship, not a woman!

He rushed to the rails. Lifeboats dotted the black horizon, their passengers incredibly difficult to make out with clarity. He swung a kerosene lantern in front of him. Its pale light only served to show how far *Titanic* had dipped into the icy ocean.

Undaunted, Weiss kept surveying the bobbing crafts. Then he saw his target. The silver-blue hair sat atop a large woman, wrapped in a heavy woolen shawl, huddled among at least sixty other passengers on the recently departed Lifeboat 6. Lou was among them.

The Agent was escaping with the Toxic.

45

Twin inevitabilities threatened to stop *Titanic*'s band from continuing to play. The first was the sinking ship itself, its bow now dipping below the waterline. A trio of brass propellers in the stern towered far in the air, assuring that the vessel had only moments left afloat before it would be pulled under.

The second was a multitude of horribly disfigured ghouls marching toward the sound of "Nearer My God, To Thee."

Wallace Hartley's violin bow did not so much as quaver.

He and his band had accepted the captain's call. *There's nothing more noble than using our God-given gifts*—that was Hartley's counsel to Mr. Krins, and those words passed the test of truth. The players provided enough distraction to allow *Titanic*'s final lifeboats to launch without being overrun by the dead-faced menace. Each musician understood he would not escape death, yet every one of the seven played on.

Wallace Hartley would never marry Maria. He would never hold her hand, kiss her lips, or see her beaming smile on Earth again. The men had nothing now but their music, which wafted through the air with the utmost serenity. They were oblivious to the carnage raging around them. Their trust in God's greater plan was total, and with this song their lives were complete. Drawn to the music like bugs to light, the fiends reached for Hartley as he applied a final, spectacular flourish to his violin and accepted the fate God had determined.

The zombies' grasp fell short. For as Hartley held his final note, *Titanic* broke in half, sending a wave of water across the deck that washed the band away from their tormentors and into the frigid sea where each man would sleep. Heroes to the last, the seven men believed God's mercy had spared them from a fate worse than death.

Captain Smith tried to wrench himself free, but the handcuffs clanked and held firm. He'd left the key in King's office for a reason. Something like a laugh escaped from his blackened mouth as he held the pegs of *Titanic*'s wheel.

When Smith had locked himself in place, the ringing in his mind had reached a sharp, shrill crescendo and then fallen away as something inside him snapped for good. Outside sounds entered his head, but what he heard was no longer recognizable as music. Screaming passengers sailed past the wheelhouse, and the sharp metal cuffs tore into Smith's wrists as he struggled to break free and chase them. Then, with a sickening lurch, he was tossed forward into the wheel as the bow dove completely underwater.

Captain Edward J. Smith was pulled directly into the Atlantic along with the front end of his finest ship, but he felt no pain, no sorrow, no regret. Only his body sank like a stone.

The deck shifted beneath Weiss's feet as *Titanic* broke in two. While the stern appeared to settle back to even keel, the bow on which Weiss was standing was nearly gone. He tightened his life jacket and backed up two steps to get a running start. With a deep breath, he sprinted for the deck's edge just before it disappeared, vaulted over the brass railing, and flung himself into the ocean.

The icy water sent an electric shock through his skull. His plunge took Weiss deep below the surface and into utter darkness. The frigid water numbed the pain in his shoulder as Weiss let the lifejacket return him to the surface. When he finally broke through, he erupted in a long spasm of sputtering gasps.

A deck chair floated next to him, and he tried to pull himself atop its wooden frame. But it did little to keep his body out of the glacial water and he abandoned it. With surprising strength, he began swimming toward Lifeboat 6.

Panicked screams surrounded him. Hundreds bobbed in the water, each person desperately searching for something to cling to as the freezing water drained all feeling from their bodies.

Where the black waterline met the night sky, lifeboats slowly rowed away from *Titanic*. Passengers pleaded with crewmen to return for those in the water. As he swam, Weiss spotted a few zombies along the surface, but to a creature, they sank like anchors. Their awkward movements were too clumsy and slow to even tread water. Weiss suspected the pressure of the deep would eventually crush the creatures' skulls into oblivion.

"Mr. Weiss!"

Weiss shook the saltwater from his eyes. Lou was waving at him from Lifeboat 6. "You can make it, Mr. Weiss!" Lou shouted. "You're doing it!"

He wasn't so sure. Even though he'd only been swimming for minutes, his arms weakened and his progress slowed. The lifeboat was perhaps fifty yards off and moving away, as its two able seamen rowed like mad. In the boat, the matron in silver-blue hair shifted and smiled in his direction.

"Lou!" Weiss shouted, hoping his voice could still carry across the water. *It has to be you; you're my last hope.* Weiss prayed she would understand, and that he was not sentencing her to death. "Fourteen trunks!" Weiss cried. "It's the lady with the fourteen trunks!"

Lou looked puzzled—perhaps Mr. Weiss had become delirious. Why was he shouting about Lady Cardeza? Was there something in one of her trunks? But no one had been allowed any luggage . . .

Lou scanned the passengers in her lifeboat, and then she understood—there was Lady Cardeza's silver-blue hair, askew as always, but it was atop the head and body of someone decidedly larger and more rugged. It was a man, in fact, hiding beneath that shawl and disguise. Mr. Weiss was alerting her to Hargraves in a way that the thief wouldn't understand.

Lou started worming her way past the other passengers to the back of boat. Hargraves seemed to be staring off elsewhere, not moving, apparently huddling against the cold. A hawk-nosed woman grabbed Lou and tried to pull her down into a seat, lecturing her on the dangers of rocking the boat. Lou escaped the woman's clutches and kept moving.

"You'll sit like you're told!" commanded McCarthy, one of the two seamen rowing the boat. He reached for Lou, but she squirted past. "There's no time for monkey play!"

Lunging out of his seat, McCarthy latched onto Lou's collar just as she reached Hargraves and snatched the blue hair from his head.

"Imposter!" Lou cried.

The other passengers gasped. "Coward!" shrieked the hawk-nosed woman. "Women and children first!"

The exposed spy calmly rose to his feet and reached inside the shawl, producing the pistol he'd stolen from Kaufmann and training it on Lou. "You are proving to be quite an irritant, young lady," the Agent said. He then swung the gun toward McCarthy, who was reaching into his vest. "Keep your hands away from that pocket, sir. I have six shots, and at this range, that means six dead."

"Hell you say!" came a shout from behind the Agent. A sharp elbow cracked the back of his head as Margaret Brown (or Molly, as her friends called her) sent the man sprawling to the deck of the lifeboat.

The gun flew from his hand, but that wasn't what caught Lou's eye. A stainless-steel cylinder also fell from beneath the Agent's woolen shawl to rattle along the lifeboat floor. Quick as a blink, Lou pounced on the Toxic before the Agent had time to recover.

"Mr. Weiss!" Lou shouted, holding the tube high above her head. "I've got it! What we've been searching for!"

A surge of hope warmed Weiss's freezing body, and he swam with renewed vigor. The impossible had happened—they'd recovered the Toxic! And the able seamen had stopped rowing, allowing Weiss to close the distance with Lifeboat 6. He might find his cure after all.

Yet Lifeboat 6 now rocked with the tussle between McCarthy and the Agent over the pistol. Then a gunshot split the air, and McCarthy clutched his gut and crumpled to his knees. The Agent trained his gun on the other able seaman before raising a foot and kicking McCarthy into the ocean.

"There will be no more heroics," hissed the Agent. He swept his weapon from the front of the boat to the back, finally training the firearm on Molly Brown. "You will not receive another warning." Then he turned the gun on Lou. "Return it now. Do you really think I won't shoot a child?"

No one else can die, Weiss thought. Even in his head, the words moved slowly. *It's time to put an end to this.*

"Lou!" called Weiss. "Throw it into the ocean!"

The Agent cocked the gun. "That," he said, "would be a very bad idea."

Lou agreed, though not because she was afraid of any gun. *Let him shoot me,* she thought, *so long as he wastes more bullets.* One day, Mr. Weiss would tell her story, and how she saved the day.

"I won't, Mr. Weiss!" Lou hollered. "You worked too hard! We all did! You can still find a cure!"

"I can't save anyone, not now," managed Weiss, shaking uncontrollably, the bitter-cold water freezing his veins. He mumbled, "But you can . . ."

"Don't be a fool," the Agent said to Lou as he inched down the lifeboat toward her. Two women fainted at the sight of the gun, while others cowered in their seats. "Return what belongs to me . . . and you will live. You have my word."

Lou cocked her arm back as if to throw a newspaper, stopping the Agent in his tracks. "Don't move!" Lou shouted. "Shoot me, and I'll send this into the water, understand?" The Agent raised his gun but didn't fire.

Then a sickening, gurgling *whooooosh* caught everyone's attention. *Titanic*'s stern, now nearly vertical, was being dragged below the surface of the Atlantic. A violent whirlpool formed as the back half of the monstrous ship sank, pulling down everything in its wake. Screams mixed with the rushing, roaring sound of the drowning vessel.

"Mr. Weiss!" Lou called. "Here's your cure!"

With a hop and a heave as mighty as she could manage, Lou sent the canister flying into the air . . . and well above Weiss, who watched the Toxic sail over his head and land dead square in the center of the suction created by *Titanic*.

"No!" shouted the Agent. In a panic, he shed his shawls and dove heedlessly into the water after the Toxic. He was a powerful swimmer, but the whirlpool sucked him deep beneath the Atlantic. He did not surface again.

Weiss looked to Lou, standing triumphant in the lifeboat. The Toxic was gone, never to be retrieved. Destroying the vial was the closest Weiss would come to a cure.

"Now swim!" shouted Lou. "Please! You can still save yourself!"

But Weiss knew that time had passed. Perhaps if he had escaped another way in the first place. Perhaps if he had sought the captain's help earlier. Perhaps . . .

Weiss whispered, "Thank you, Lou." He could barely see the boat.

"We can make room for you, there's room!" Lou pleaded, tears in her eyes. "But you gotta swim!"

Weiss was too tired for swimming.

"Go back for him!" Lou begged the seaman with the oars.

Weiss lay back in the water and found his sister in the night sky. He tried to speak, but Sabine shushed him with a pale finger to his blue lips. Then, as if she were sitting in the crook of a branch in their favorite climbing tree, she held out her hand.

Weiss's life-jacket was slowly pulled back into the suction. He unbuckled the vest and reached up. Something like the afternoon sun blinded him, and he felt unburdened. Theodor Weiss closed his eyes as his twin pulled him to a higher place.

Lou stared at the spot where Weiss disappeared, waiting for him to resurface. The girl held her breath and counted silently in her head, not knowing how many seconds a man could stay underwater before needing to breathe again. Near three hundred, she inhaled sharply, gulping the night air. Then she sat and fought back tears, determined not to cry because it never made things any better.

The ocean was smooth and black. The screams of the poor souls still trapped in the frigid water soon dissipated altogether. Other lifeboats littered the horizon, but Lou could see no liner coming to their rescue. Some lady in the back of the boat was sobbing. The remaining seaman put a comforting hand on Lou's shoulder. The hook-nosed woman tried to put a blanket around the girl but she shrugged it off. She wanted to feel the cold.

No one said a word.

46

Senator William Alden Smith of Michigan asked several questions about the nature of the collision and exactly how fast *Titanic* was traveling, but J. Bruce Ismay claimed limited knowledge of such things.

In fact, he still appeared to be in shock. His eyes only met the senator's to express profound grief over the lives lost in the terrible disaster. In a voice barely above a whisper, Ismay claimed that he was only a passenger, just like all the others enjoying *Titanic*'s maiden voyage, and he had insufficient knowledge to explain the hows and whys of the tragedy.

"Just an ordinary passenger?" Senator Smith repeated skeptically.

The head of the White Star line claimed to have no idea the ship had an inadequate supply of lifeboats. He further went on to say that he never ordered anyone to push *Titanic* up to full speed.

Senator Smith turned his attention to Ismay's rescue. The court stenographer noted their exchange:

SENATOR SMITH: *What were the circumstances, Mr. Ismay, of your departure from the ship?*

MR. ISMAY: *In what way?*

SENATOR SMITH: *Did the last boat that you went on leave the ship from some point near where you were?*

MR. ISMAY: *I was immediately opposite the lifeboat when she left.*

SENATOR SMITH: *Immediately opposite?*

MR. ISMAY: *Yes.*

SENATOR SMITH: *What were the circumstances of your departure from the ship? I ask merely that . . .*

MR. ISMAY: *The boat was there. There was a certain number of men in the boat, and the officer called out asking if there were any more women, and there was no response, and there were no passengers left on the deck.*

SENATOR SMITH: *There were no passengers on the deck?*

MR. ISMAY: *No, sir; and as the boat was in the act of being lowered away, I got into it.*

SENATOR SMITH: *Naturally, you would remember that if you saw it? When you entered the lifeboat yourself, you say there were no passengers on that part of the ship?*

MR. ISMAY: *None.*

SENATOR SMITH: *Did you, at any time, see any struggle among the men to get into these boats?*

MR. ISMAY: *No.*

SENATOR SMITH: *Was there any attempt, as this boat was being lowered past the other decks, to have you take on more passengers?*

MR. ISMAY: *None, sir. There were no passengers there to take on.*

The senator motioned for the stenographer to stop documenting the proceedings. He approached Ismay and paused a long moment before continuing.

"And now, Mr. Ismay, off the record," he said. "Is there anything else you'd care to discuss? The committee has heard certain rumors, several of them of a particularly disturbing nature."

Ismay's eyes looked haunted. "I've spoken about all I know," he said hoarsely. "The event was a horror. Everyone sees things differently in such total chaos, and memories of terror are usually the flimsiest. The mind is desperate to move on—and for good reason."

Senator Smith knew then he would never get any more truth from J. Bruce Ismay.

The inquiry went on for seventeen more days, but outside the hotel, New York's daily papers were already passing judgment.

"Coward of the Century!" hawked a newsboy, holding up a paper with a picture of a defeated Ismay for all to see.

A young girl stopped to read the headline. She was about the same age as the newsboy, with a skinned nose, worn skirt, and rusty hair. She flipped a coin in the air and took a copy of the paper to read later.

While walking down the bustling streets of New York, she stared at the faces as they passed by, one after another, bright and full of life. She was ready to journey to Iowa, to start her own life anew and grateful for the chance.

EPILOGUE

"Nervous?" Maggie Liu asked. The attractive director of entertainment for Las Vegas's Zephyr Casino held a clipboard in her right arm. "We're looking forward to a huge run."

The Man in Red laughed. "Nervous? Me? Never. We're ready to go. You know what *Titanic Resurrected*'s numbers were in Vancouver? And in Nashville and San Francisco?"

Maggie smiled. "I do. That's why you're here. Zephyr only wants the biggest shows. We only bet sure things. Maybe you've heard, but in Vegas, the house *always* wins."

"I have heard that, but the great thing is there's no way we can lose. Let me show you why."

For the next half hour, as his crew feverishly bolted the plywood platforms and polished the Plexiglas displays, the Man in Red gave Maggie the grand tour, winding through historically accurate recreations of a first-class passenger suite, an elaborate dining hall, the grand staircase, and case after case of artifacts that had been raised from the wreck. Billed as "a historical voyage of romance and intrigue!" *Titanic Resurrected* was massive in scope and scale, the biggest collection of *Titanic* artifacts ever gathered. Tomorrow was the 100th anniversary of the *Titanic*'s sinking, and the Man in Red had planned a special event to mark the occasion.

"So, this is the big mystery?" Maggie asked, walking over to a finished Plexiglas display. Inside, positioned in a satin-lined case, was a cylindrical, stainless-steel container. "Doesn't look like much."

"We know something's inside. Scans showed a smaller, liquid-filled tube, probably glass. I've had the top *Titanic* experts weigh in, and no one recognizes it or knows what it might have been used for. We'll find out tomorrow when we uncork it."

"Won't it be a big disappointment if it's only ink or water or something boring?"

"Well, the show's run is almost sold out already, and the pay-per-view is going gangbusters, so we make money either way. But ultimately that's not what interests me. Whatever it is, we'll learn something."

"Yeah right—like anyone learns anything in this town." Maggie laughed.

"You're about to learn something right now," he said, lifting a key ring dangling from a belt loop and unlocking the back of the case.

"What do you mean?" Maggie responded.

"What, you think I haven't opened the cylinder before?" The Man in Red grinned. "Do you want to see it or not?"

Maggie gave him a practiced, casual nod.

The Man in Red reached in, carefully lifting out the stainless-steel cylinder. "The only thing I won't do is open the vial," he warned. "Don't tell anyone I did this for you."

As his hand wrapped around the top of the canister to unscrew it, the floor began to shake. He stopped short and looked over at Maggie.

"Just a little earthquake," she said with an easy smile. "Nothing to worry about. This property is more than a match for a tremor like that."

"Fine for your casino," said the Man in Red. "I have priceless displays of china and crystal to worry about." He quickly placed the cylinder back into the display case.

"Wait here. I'll be right back," he told Maggie, and then he ran off to check his other displays.

Maggie slyly glanced around. He'd left the case unlocked, and no one was watching. She grabbed the cylinder, spun the cap off, gazed inside, and frowned. Turning the cylinder upside down, a much smaller glass tube slid into her waiting hand. She put the cylinder down.

Staring at the jet-black fluid inside the tube, she shook her head, unimpressed—*a bunch of ink, that's all. Some big mystery.*

Then her phone rang. Impatiently, she set the glass tube on a neighboring table, turned around, and answered the call.

As she did, a mild aftershock shook Las Vegas. The table behind her wobbled, and the tube rolled slowly toward the edge.